I0762408

MOTHER MERCY

CHANDRA ARTHUR

INIMITABLE BOOKS
UNFORGETTABLE STORIES

Published by Inimitable Books, LLC
www.inimitablebooks.com

Library of Congress Cataloguing-in-Publication Data is available.

First edition, 2026
Cover design by Christian Storm

ISBN 978-1-958607-49-7 (hardcover)
10 9 8 7 6 5 4 3 2 1

To the villains:
I hope you die screaming.

THESE CASES CONTAIN

Animal cruelty (implied, not on the page)
Child abuse
Child sexual assault
Death
Domestic abuse
Dismemberment
Emetophobia triggers
Gore
Human trafficking
Murder
Mutilation
Physical abuse
Psychological abuse
Rape/sexual assault
Religious abuse
Spousal abuse
Stalking
Substance abuse
Torture

If there are any updates or changes to the list, you can check out chandraarthur.com for the most up-to-date version.

DISCLAIMER

This book is not intended as an instruction manual. The activities described in this novel are solely intended for narrative purposes.

While I am an IT professional, some of the actions described in this book are purely theoretical on my part. This is partly because they are not the focus of my career, but primarily because they are not necessary for me to perform my job. And I'm not committing crimes.

While there are legitimate uses for some real methods described within these pages, they should not be used lightly. Please do not attempt the actions in this book on your own. There are real-world cybersecurity risks and other dangerous things that you can expose yourself to if you don't know what you're doing.

Additionally, do not follow my protagonist's actions as a road map. I am not advocating anyone take up a life of crime.

If you are also an IT professional, thank you for reading this. There is a chance that what I'm referencing to is within your wheelhouse. I love that for you, and hope you enjoy my story and the creative license I've taken.

Mark Eric Ballinger, aged 31, passed away unexpectedly on June 5, 1987, at his home in Rapidan, Virginia. He was born on April 5, 1956, to Mr. and Mrs. Jefferson Ballinger.

A private service will be held at the family estate.

-Obituary, published June 9, 1987

BETH

PROLOGUE

Pink brain matter speckled the harvest gold refrigerator. Darker spots of blood splatter fill in the macabre canvas. The house was quiet. *Finally.*

Poppy limped into the kitchen, still favoring her paw.

Beth scooped her up before she walked into the mess. The beagle licked her cheek, then blew puppy breath into her face.

The tears came all at once. Not *sad* tears, but the kind that mixed shock and relief. She'd thought it might come to this, but Beth hadn't expected it to be so soon.

She pushed down the rolling waves of emotion that were fizzing inside her. She didn't have time to deal with them now. She cleared her throat, then carried Poppy down the hall to the bathroom, where the dog would be safe, and closed the door.

There wasn't time to clean everything up. The blood was already starting to seep into the grout between the tiles.

People would know who had done it, anyway. There was no way she could bury two hundred and fifty pounds of a dead man by herself.

It would have taken her a week just to dig the hole. All the while, his body would be blocking access to the kitchen.

A woman could hardly be expected to do that kind of backbreaking labor on an empty stomach.

She could feel the hysterical laughter tickling the back of her throat.

No, there wasn't time.

Everyone had seen the bruises, and no one had tried—bothered—to do anything. It had been a family matter until she pulled the trigger.

Now, there was a thin margin between self-defense and homicide.

Sure, she could wait around and plead her case, but she knew how that would go around here. His cousins were the commonwealth's attorney and the chief of police, and his uncle was the only judge in the county. There wasn't a fair shake to be had in this town. Not for love or money. And she had neither. Well, not love. She had a little money and a pamphlet with the name of a place for women like her.

The clock on the nightstand read *10:30*.

If Mark wasn't at the diner by noon, they'd start calling the house. Once they called, if someone didn't answer, she'd have ten—maybe fifteen—minutes.

The door of what had been their bedroom stood open at the end of the hall. The bed was still unmade.

She pulled her suitcase down from the top shelf in the small closet and dumped the rolled sweaters onto the floor to make space for the things she would need.

Down the hall, Poppy whined from within the bathroom, scratching at the closed door. Beth ignored her. She couldn't have her baby tainted by his blood. Besides, now that it was just the two of them, no one would be angry anymore if the puppy peed on the floor.

Beth rolled seven pairs of underwear, socks, two pairs of jeans, and two simple dresses. She placed them into the empty suitcase. Then she pulled a winter coat, raincoat, and sweater from the closet on their hangers and stuffed them into her garment bag. She didn't have much that she wanted to take with her, but there still wasn't a lot of space.

Marriage license, birth certificate, social security card, driver's license, and the title to the car. The family photo album, minus the picture of her and Mark in front of the diner.

She wasn't sure why, but she felt weird leaving it behind.

After slinging her purse over her shoulder, she felt around inside for the keys. Nothing.

Shit.

They had to be in his pocket.

At least the car was unlocked.

Carefully stepping over the spreading pool of blood that was coming from the kitchen, she carried the suitcase to the car first. Then the garment bag.

Back in the bedroom, she pulled open the top drawer of her dresser just enough so she could run her hand along the underside of the top, feeling for the tab of tape she had put there months ago.

This was her safe haven. The one place she would be able to start over. She slipped the card into her purse, then moved her nightstand away from the wall and shifted the loose baseboard so she could fit her hand into the gap between the studs.

The cash was stashed in four cardboard toilet-paper rolls. She wasn't sure how much, but it would have to be enough. She stuffed them into her purse.

She pushed everything back out of the way and tried to decide what to do next. Move his body to get the keys or get her toiletries and Poppy from the bathroom?

She decided on the keys.

If she got blood on her, she'd have to shower, and it was too hot for Poppy to sit in the car while she got cleaned up.

Shit.

She'd forgotten to pack Poppy's stuff. Her baby's bed, toys, food, and bowls all needed to go into the car.

Then she'd have to get the keys.

Beth hadn't really looked at him since she shot him. Granted, there wasn't much to see. The top of his head was just *gone*, and the rest of his brain leaked out when his heart stopped.

He was slumped forward, his back propped against the fridge, keeping him from sliding to the floor. Her keys were in his front pocket, where he'd stashed them right after he pushed her into the wall, choked her, and punched her in the face.

She played it again in her head.

Going limp, sliding down to the floor, waiting for the kick in the ribs. She took in the silence, listening for the sound, the seal on the fridge giving way, him searching for his pre-lunch beer.

His eyes went wide when he turned.

She pulled the trigger.

The keys were sealed safely in his pocket, pinned in the hip crease. There was no way she could unfold him to reach them. She'd never tried to move a body before, and he was already starting to go stiff. Or maybe it was the dead weight.

She reached for the kitchen scissors, clipped through the thick denim of his pants with the boning shears, and pulled the keys free. Then she checked her clothes for blood. Not too bad.

Beth glanced at the clock on the stove again. *11:00.*

Poppy had peed on the bathroom's pink rug. She wagged her tail and yapped happily at her owner.

Stepping around Poppy's mess, Beth grabbed her makeup, toiletry case, and the drugstore bag with detergent in it. She opened the empty washing soda box and checked that the three packages of hair dye were still inside, then scooped Poppy up to take her to the car.

Beth tossed her stuff onto the back floorboard, got in, and started the car. The speakers blasted a new radio hit that was way too loud and cheerful. Beth turned it down to a background murmur.

Poppy snuffled at her face as she leaned across to roll the passenger window down. She left the driver's side rolled down, too, then ran back inside for one more thing.

She wadded up some paper towels and stuffed them into the toaster. Next, she made a trail of paper and tablecloth and pinned it in place with the wooden cutting board. She grabbed the mower gas can from the back porch, which she used to douse the living room, hall, and lastly—Mark on the linoleum floor.

She walked around the kitchen island and leaned across the counter to press start on the toaster, and waited just long enough to see the paper begin to smoke. She threw the can to the ground to be eaten by the growing flames, then stepped out onto the porch again and closed the door behind her for the last time.

Back in the car, the dash clock read *11:30*.

Beth put the vehicle in gear, then backed out of the driveway and turned the vehicle away from town. She waited on the edge of the curb for a few more minutes 'til she could see the glow of fire inside the house, then she shifted into drive and pulled away.

By the time she made it to the county road, wisps of black smoke were already curling up to the sky. She pulled onto the shoulder, making way for a fire truck, and looked at the clock. Back at the house, she was sure the phone was ringing.

Noon.

ABBY

ONE

There are seven parts to a job:

1. Getting the target: Percilla sends a dossier with the details.
2. Setup and surveillance: I scope out the area.
3. Confirmation and planning: Witness the crime and determine the appropriate punishment.
4. The kill.
5. The escape.
6. Lying low: my least favorite part of any job.
7. And reset to do it all again.

Right now, I'm at dreaded number six, especially because the last job was pretty messy and I'm 'supposed to be doing nothing' until the story dies down.

But this new piece of information in my head is eating at me.

Yesterday, after she's refused to give me a new case for *weeks*, I told Percilla that I knew where Mom was buried. When I was home weeks ago, I found the newspaper clipping she had been hiding.

The only problem is, Mom's not buried there anymore.

I scrub my hands over my face, rubbing the sleep from my eyes. *I need a shower.*

The drive from Dallas hasn't been bad, but I'm tired of going nowhere. I would give almost anything to be on another assignment.

Instead of killing time in Louisiana, I'd rather be helping someone. It takes time to set up a job correctly, and when I'm hiding out, just sitting on my hands—I know there's a cost.

I don't try to find a truck stop with good showers. Instead, I look for a small gym. The kind of place that is less likely to have cameras. I get a day pass and bathe there. When I'm done getting dressed, I head back to the van, grab a granola bar, and open my laptop.

I navigate to the most recent file. A copy of a newspaper clipping with a story about my mother's death. Not all identifying information has been removed.

I clench my jaw and squeeze my eyes shut. I didn't say half of what I was thinking when we last talked about it. I still hadn't told her how much I remembered. When she came to get me, Percilla was wearing a floral dress with buttons down the front. She took me out of the house–had *dragged* me because I hadn't wanted to leave Mom, her mousy brown hair stuck to the floor with blood. *Too much blood.* I had tried to cover the hole in her head.

I open my eyes and force myself to focus.

I roll the storage chest out from under my bed, one of the three that form the bulk of my storage. My carefully organized life, all stowed neatly away. I store most of my tech in here so I can access it easily without getting out of the van. I grab a new burner phone and slide the clean computer into the empty slot in the Faraday cage, where I keep all my laptops. I slide the bin closed.

The phone number for the shelter is ingrained in my memory. I dial, listening to it ring.

"You have reached Mother Mercy Ministries. If you know your party's extension, please enter it now. If this is an emergency, press zero. Otherwise, please wait on the line for assistance."

I enter the extension for Percilla's office. After it rings five times, she answers.

"Abby." She's still upset I let things get so messy in Arkansas. I can tell from her dry tone, even though she doesn't say it.

Maybe for the first time, Amity has made national news. That is never great, but the authorities haven't been able to associate me with any of it. Apparently, there are a lot of people who wanted Andrew Clark dead.

"I read the article you hid from me, the one about Mom. There are some details missing."

She's quiet for a long time, but I wait.

"I don't think you understand what you're asking me to do. I'm sorry I couldn't save your mother, but that doesn't mean I'm going to send you to your death to make you feel better. I'm not saying I'll never tell you. I'm saying 'not now.' You're not ready."

"I deserve to know the truth!"

"You know more than enough already."

"Yes, I know what happened that day. I was *there*, Percilla. I remember. The house where mom and I lived was put on the market a few months ago. But what I don't know is where the rest of my family is. The courthouse that had Mom's marriage certificate burned down with everything inside it."

I've done a lot of research in my downtime. But with the public records being destroyed, there's not a lot I can find.

After Arkansas, I drove to the closest border, which happened to be Texas, then headed back east through Louisiana and Alabama. I could just go to where my mom was buried, look at the empty hole in the ground. If I stay on I20 all the way to Atlanta, convince myself I'm going to head north and spend some time camping in the Nantahala National Forest.

But I don't have to decide about Virginia 'til I reach Georgia.

That will take at least two days given how fast I'm driving.

"Your mother was your family. You came from her. You are everything good she ever was and more. You get to live and make the world a better place."

"So, that's it, then? You're not going to tell me?"

She huffs out a slow breath, but doesn't say anything.

"I can't sit around like this anymore. I need to work. If you won't be honest with me, at least let me help other people."

"Fine. I'll get something for you. Check back this afternoon."

"I love you," I say through clenched teeth.

She laughs, but I can hear the tears in her voice when she says it back to me.

Then the line goes dead.

TWO

Getting the job is the easy part, but what takes the most skill is the setup and planning. While it would be fun—maybe even easy—to run in guns blazing, it would definitely get me caught. And maybe get other people killed. That's why I have my process.

I have to be sure who the abuser is. I have to *see* it. It's the only way that I can be the judge, jury, and executioner. I will not shed innocent blood. It's bad enough that there are people who have done nothing wrong already locked in cells. Not to mention those who've received the death penalty, only to be posthumously exonerated.

And I have to know what the abuser is capable of so I don't end up being another one of their victims.

I can't help anyone if I'm dead.

I have to make sure the victim is out of the house. I'm not equipped to deal with a hostage situation. And I don't want to force them into a position where they have to lie on the witness stand.

I also don't want the victim to be a suspect. They must have an alibi for when their abuser meets their end.

I have ten laptops. Five different colors, each with their own purpose, so nothing gets mixed up. And each color has two laptops. One primary and one backup.

Silver is personal.

On the occasions when I watch movies or shop for anything, I use that. While I try to stay off the internet, it's good to have a laptop where I don't do anything related to my work. I also try to keep these a little longer. Sometimes, I even put a few stickers on them for fun. It's one of the only ways I express myself. Every other outlet tends to stand out too much. Sometimes I'll order items and have them delivered to a shelter. No one would think twice about that, but I'm really particular about my shampoo. The one I use doesn't have a lot of fragrance, plus the conditioner leaves my hair soft and easy to detangle. But I'm not risking going into a major store with all the cameras corporate money can buy just so I can get more of it.

Black is for Tor, the only browser I use. It doesn't have the same tracking features other browsers have, and it allows me to use some other dark web tools that just aren't compatible with your average search engine. And it's the only one that works with SecureDrop, which is what Percilla uses to send me files.

Dear Mother,

I know you get a lot of these. I can't imagine I'm very high on your list, but if you could find it in your heart to help me, I would be forever grateful. I have no one else to turn to, and I'm afraid. I can't live like this anymore. I'm not safe here. but I have no place to go. He's hurting me.

The last time, I ended up in the hospital, and I'm afraid next time, it will be worse.

Corrin

I don't know exactly how Percilla gets the letters, but when she does, she uploads them with a dossier of all the details she can get for me and all the information I need to track down my target.

After downloading the folder, I move it to my thumb drive, log out, and shut the black computer down.

Then I switch to a white laptop.

I move the folder from the flash drive to my desktop, then disconnect the USB before I plug in a second thumb drive that carries the decryption key. Once the file is decrypted, I put both thumb drives back in the small lockbox I keep them in.

White is clean, offline, and boring. This is where I transfer, decrypt, and read the files I download from SecureDrop. White laptops never go on any network. Before I start using one, I also open up the back and remove the wireless card, just to be sure. When the job is done, I remove all the files from the device. If I needed to destroy one completely for any reason, it wouldn't be the worst thing.

I open the couple's details.

The first item in the file is their photo. Aiden Lancaster the third next to his wife Corrin. *Of course he's a Third.* It immediately marks him as an endearing figure in a punchable-face sort of way.

Some of the photos look like they came from happier times. In one, the couple stands in front of a flashy new-construction house, the classic Alabama suburb style of new money that's rich but not rich enough to afford one of the old money houses.

Maybe I'm imagining it, but I can see a hollow expression already forming behind her eyes. I skim through the pictures, looking for floor plans and schedules. She is a housewife, but there are no kids. Thank goodness for that. Jobs with children are a thousand times harder.

He has his own office building. It's for day trading or crypto—whatever that means—but it looks more like a college frat boy's post-dropout investment. Only this one actually succeeded. Maybe. It's too soon to tell if mommy and daddy's money is keeping it afloat.

His schedule is precise.

I expected him to be sloppy like most of the frat boys I've seen, but he is fastidious. His company seems to be profitable, and he's well connected in the area. The Gulf in Alabama is known for engineering. Big homes, finance, and expensive hobbies. It seems that his investments fall in that space and the businesses he is connected with are built around his aesthetic.

They have a big boat. Not as big as some of their friends, but it's still a statement piece. Her ring cost almost as much as the house, though it looks like her car was where he saved some cash. The SUV, the truck (because it's Alabama, obviously), and a sporty car seem to be mostly for show. That doesn't even count the utility vehicles for hunting, or the land leases, and out-of-state hunting trips. Because they own a speedboat, they also appear to regularly schedule deep-sea fishing trips.

The key here is picking a time when they can't travel far—and with their money, they have a lot of options for quick trips. All of those vacation options would make it impossible for me to follow them. If he takes her out of state, I'll have to start again. From scratch.

Next will be getting familiar with where they go and when.

Percilla is good.

She has included a list of their regular commutes and average drive times.

But I still need more information.

Gray laptops are for research. There's no reason behind that color other than most cheap laptops are gray, and I go through them quickly. I don't usually have any questions 'til I'm finished reading through the information Percilla sends me, but I keep my research laptop on hand while I go through the dossier so I can map things out as I go.

I do not sign into any accounts or connect to any network for work that I have ever connected to on a personal laptop. Paranoid? Yes. Overkill? Maybe. But I've found that being a little over the top about security is never a bad thing. There's always someone smarter who can figure out a pattern, even the ones I don't intentionally create. So,

I try my best to make sure there isn't much crossover. I can't have my cases connected.

Before I start on anything else, I need to ensure I can get out quickly if something goes sideways. Even if I'm just feeling jumpy. I can always come back once the coast is clear.

Then I research the places they go, those locations' busy hours, and which spots are under surveillance. Ideally, the victim should be at one of those venues while I'm taking care of the abuser.

For this case, I have the most questions about travel times and which routes are the busiest. I check for traffic cameras and build an escape plan.

Of course, I'll set up my own surveillance. If I have to connect to someone's internet network to access any of their accounts, it's going on a red laptop. Because it's hot, in other words, it's as close to legal danger as I'm comfortable getting.

I always dump them after a job.

I review my research one more time. It's enough. Now, it's time to make a plan.

CORRIN

THREE

Aiden and Corrin's neighborhood isn't gated, which isn't unusual around here, even for houses this size. The community has a faux gate with the neighborhood name on it, but it's more of a city beautification project than a source of security.

I find a place to park near a utility access area, place some cones, and settle in to work.

It's odd that, given all the news around security, *some* people still feel the need to run security cameras in their homes directed at their living space, connected to an unsecured network named *The Lancasters*, often with the distinctive password: *Password.*

There's no two-factor authentication in place, and the firmware hasn't been updated in so long that the vulnerabilities are well-documented and easy to exploit. I'm half-tempted to update their devices when I'm done, but it would only be for my amusement if I did.

I spend some time getting familiar with the house and how they operate. I'd love to see their calendars, but I'm not about to clone a phone. When they eventually pull his cell cite data to piece together what led up to what's about to happen, I don't want his location traceable anywhere near me.

It doesn't take me long to get comfortable with the house and the camera setup. He's been thorough with the surveillance coverage of the floor plan. It's nice for me, but kinda stupid of him, considering he's taken so few precautions with digital security.

I got in. And I'm not even that good.

Once I'm familiar with the layout, I'll shadow them to see what's been going on and if it's as bad as she said it is. I like to believe women, but I've learned two rules from experience. "Trust, but verify," and "Measure twice, cut once." *Both sayings apply in my line of work.*

They don't always make it this easy, but the bird's-eye view has given me the option to try something new, my own version of on-the-job training. It's important to keep things fresh, not just to ensure I don't develop a clear signature, but also because it's good to have range. Since, situations are straightforward and simple, I can practice then. So when things get complicated, you have somewhere to take it.

I start by measuring his height using the camera angle, the picture frame on the wall, and an average room with vaulted ceilings. New construction is prone to settling. Given that the building schematic says the hallway is fifteen feet long, it's fairly easy to refine that number and figure out where his neck will be.

As a woman, there are some things that go against my personal inclination. For example, I'd much rather use poison. But it is, by nature, unreliable. Put in too much, and maybe they purge all the contents from their stomachs. Too little, and they are able to survive with medical intervention.

And you never know when someone will change their usual routine, skip breakfast or share a sip of coffee with a friend. Maybe they give the cup to someone. They could toss the liquid, spill it, or leave it on top of their car.

No, toxins aren't reliable.

It's far better to stick with what you can control. Most of the time, that means doing the work yourself.

But I don't mind taking a hands-on approach. And when you're small and have to worry about being overpowered, you get ideas. What had always been my biggest concern became a strength. And one thing I've realized is that abusers aren't that smart. Yes, they are often charming, but since I don't give a shit about that, it's a lot easier for me to see through them.

I think about that. Part of what made 2020 so bad was that there was no one to witness who people really were behind closed doors. Victims were stuck at home with their abusers.

And I hadn't started working yet.

Understanding how horrible people hide how evil they are has made me better at my job.

When Percilla doesn't have me benched.

Given all of that, I like to use things that are consistent.

Airway. Breathing. Circulation.

I fight the urge to reread the newspaper clipping I found.

No wonder she was happy to give me a job now.

She knows I can't leave someone defenseless.

FOUR

Corrin is tough as nails. Only a week into watching her complete her grueling daily routine, and I am already exhausted.

She and Aiden have already been married for three years, although I can't say for sure how long they have been living like this. With their lifestyle, my guess is that vacations don't do her much good, since she's so busy choreographing every aspect of his routine.

The light in the primary bathroom flips on at exactly five in the morning. She doesn't spend long in there.

When she comes down, she is already dressed for the day, wearing a pink and white floral pin tuck shirt with light-wash jean shorts and a pair of wedges laced with fabric that matches her top.

~~5 AM – Wake up, shower, makeup~~

She flips the light on in the kitchen and pulls a food scale out of the drawer, then takes down two mugs. She dons an apron, then measures the coffee beans out, and pours them into the grinder.

I reach for the volume and turn it down as she starts the machine and wait for her to finish before I turn the sound back up. Through the van window, I watch her come outside to get the paper. When she goes back inside the house, I return my attention to the screen.

She checks her watch, then sets a timer, before opening the fridge and reaching for the eggs and bacon.

My stomach starts rumbling just from looking at the ingredients.

She places a cast iron pan on the gas burner, but doesn't turn it on. Next, she presses the start button on the electric kettle and pours in purified water from the pitcher on the counter. She folds the paper coffee filter and fits it into the glass carafe.

I glance back at the stove, willing her to not forget it. *Don't forget to turn on the stove.*

She puts the newspaper at the head of the table before adding two full place settings.

While waiting for the water to boil, she pulls a lined notepad from the drawer by the fridge and starts making a list. She periodically glances at the coffee pot.

The kettle chimes, alerting her that the water is boiling. She pours a little over the filter, letting it rinse out the paper taste before dumping the water out, adding the coffee, and more fresh water. This time, letting it saturate the grounds.

She finally turns the stove on, letting it start to heat the pan as she adds three strips of cold bacon. After washing her hands, she finishes adding the hot water to the grounds, moving the kettle in a circle as she tips the contents out.

My stomach growls just imagining the scent of the bacon that is starting to bubble now.

She turns back to the island where the eggs are waiting, her muscle memory kicking in as she grabs a bowl, fork, shredded cheese, salt, and pepper. She cracks the eggs into the bowl, tosses the shells and washes her hands.

I reach for a granola bar and peel the foil packet open before taking an unsatisfying bite. The store was out of the good ones with peanut butter. The chewy fruit and soggy nuts are especially sad.

She is pouring coffee when Aiden comes into the kitchen. She finishes quickly, smiling at him as she offers him a cup.

He takes it from her, presses a perfunctory kiss to her cheek, and stifles a yawn.

"I turned on the towel warmer for you," she directs the comment at his back as he starts up the stairs.

We both glance at our clocks. I am really starting to get into her head. Already sure of what she will do next.

She whisks the eggs, adding salt, pepper, and a sprinkle of cheese, then flips the bacon that is sizzling in the pan. She fills a glass with orange juice, lines a plate with some paper towels, and places it next to the bacon.

The next fifteen minutes are the trickiest.

She pulls a pre-measured bowl of yogurt from the fridge and weighs it once more for good measure, forking the bacon onto the paper-lined plate and draining some of the bacon grease from the cast iron, before adding the egg mixture. She stirs it quickly.

Then she tops the yogurt with a packet of fruit and a sprinkle of granola. She stirs the eggs. And grabs a second dish of berries. Stir the eggs once more. Next, she moves the fruit to a new bowl.

6:15.

She starts moving everything onto a bamboo tray, then wipes her hands on her apron. She puts the eggs on a fresh plate, slides the bacon from the paper towel next to it, then adds the dish of fruit.

At her seat in the breakfast nook, she places the small measured parfait. At Aiden's seat, she places the bacon, eggs, fruit, and orange juice, then covers it with a gold tray topper.

Coffee, I think at her, like she can pick up the thought telepathically.

She takes the empty tray back to the kitchen, stowing it in the cabinet. She grabs her small cup of coffee and the pitcher that holds the rest of the coffee from the warmer.

She sets it down on the buffet near the breakfast table.

Apron.

She stands, untying the strings around her waist. She quickly wads up the food-stained fabric and stows it in one of the buffet drawers. She sits down again, just as Aiden strolls in.

He is wearing a teal polo, salmon-colored shorts, and loafers.

"I think I'd like to have pancakes tomorrow morning. I've got an intense boxing session in the afternoon. Any big plans for the day?"

"The usual," she says, already getting up from the table with a smile. "I do have a doctor's appointment scheduled next week."

She says it so casually, but I think there's something more to it that I'm not seeing.

Aiden stiffens, then sets his fork down. "I'll have to take off work. You know the rules. You're not going alone."

"No," she says. "Of course not."

Her nervous laugh makes me want to punch something.

Someone.

Aiden.

~~6 AM – Coffee and breakfast~~

She loads the dishwasher, wipes down the counter and appliances, cleans the grease splatters off the stove, and sprays down the sink. After checking the pantry and fridge, she tosses a few things and adds some items to her grocery list.

~~7 AM – Clean the kitchen~~

The first stop is to pick up and drop off the dry-cleaning.

Today's appointments run longer because she also gets her nails done. Judging from her hands, she goes regularly.

I'd guess every two weeks.

She heads to the grocery store, which is made more efficient since she has a list. It looks like she goes every day to keep the produce in the house picture-perfect. By the time she gets home, I'm sure she's starving. But the groceries have to be put away. She doesn't just sort the items into the fridge and pantry. She preps the fruits and veggies first. There will be no onion skin in the drawers, and the grapes come off the vine.

She has a pair of Aiden's shoes that need to be polished and a few collared shirts to be steamed. There's a bit of laundry that needs to be washed, dried, and put away.

~~8 AM – Errands and appointments~~

I watch her add half a frozen banana, some frozen blueberries, a white powder that I'm guessing is protein, and some skim milk to the blender. She lets it blend for a moment, then adds some spinach.

It looks disgusting.

She drinks it straight from the blender while standing over the sink, then she fills a cup with water and takes a few different supplements, including a prenatal vitamin.

I pause, my iced coffee halfway to my lips.

She carries the glass of water and the pills in her hand up to the primary bathroom.

An alarm on her phone goes off while she's in the bathroom.

When she comes back down, she tosses the empty vitamin bottle into the half-filled trash can, but she doesn't tie up the bag.

The housekeeper comes tomorrow.

She places both the blender and her glass into the dishwasher.

~~12 PM – Smoothie~~

She gets to start her chores a bit early. Today, she's scrubbing baseboards and doing a deep clean of the primary bathroom. I can't see much since I don't have a camera in the bathroom. I may be a killer, but I'm not a creep. But she has the door open and, from the glimpses I do catch, it looks like she's being thorough.

~~1 PM – Chores~~

It doesn't take her long to change and get ready for her run. She wears dark yoga pants, a racerback sports bra, and a tank top. Her smartwatch is fresh off the charger, and she has in a pair of earbuds.

The route she typically runs is about five miles.

There's no reason to leave my parking spot. I'll be right here when she returns.

~~2 PM – Exercise/run~~

When she gets back, she heads for the shower and comes down looking refreshed. Her hair is done, so she won't have to worry about it later, but it's up and out of her face since she still has work to do in the kitchen.

She weighs out her yogurt for the next morning and portions out fruit. She measures out the ingredients for the pancakes he requested, but doesn't combine them. Then, she slices extra veggies that go into the freezer. Everything is packed flat in a bag, labeled and dated.

~~3 PM – Shower and meal prep~~

She starts dinner right on time, switching from meal prep to blending spices, and checking her notes in the cookbook before moving to the next step. She's making steak tips and pasta. The water is already in the pot, the stove is on low, and the cast iron is preheating. She shreds half a block of cheese so she has everything ready to go but doesn't start cooking the meat or noodles yet.

~~4 PM – Cooking~~

She makes a small tray with deli-sliced prosciutto, fig jam, with space next to it for cheese. That goes into the fridge, but she leaves out the brie wedges to soften. The charcuterie tray is so artfully crafted, it took up most of her prep time. She's set out some crostini, too. That will go on the board right when she gets it out of the fridge.

With just a few minutes left, she runs upstairs to put on some makeup. She doesn't do a lot, but she does draw out her features with a bold red lip, black eyeliner, and mascara on her dark lashes.

Once she comes back downstairs, she starts on his drink, an old fashioned. She spritzes the edge of the glass with an orange peel and is pouring the cocktail as Aiden pulls into the driveway. She takes the tray back out of the fridge and adds the crostini.

She heads for the garage door, stopping at the laundry room to get him the padded slip-on shoes he wears around the house.

Corrin smiles and gives him a kiss.

He doesn't say thank you when he takes the drink from her hand and heads into his office.

Apparently, it's been a rough game of golf.

~~5 PM – Charcuterie, makeup, pre-dinner cocktails, meet Aiden at the door with slippers, a drink, and a smile~~

She turns the stove on to boil the water and lays out the bowl of cheese she grated earlier. She sets the table for two, then opens a bottle of red and pours it into a decanter to let it breathe. She places tapers and matches in the center of the table, ready to light.

She sears the steak, then lets it cook. The pasta goes into the salted water, which is now at a rolling boil.

I can see it's all coming together, but she's running low on time, and it's a toss-up as to what will upset him more—overcooked steak, or having dinner a little late.

When she re-enters the dining room, she's not wearing her apron, and she's managed to slip into a pair of black pumps. She gets dinner on the table with no time to spare.

~~6 PM – Set the table and plate dinner~~

Aiden doesn't finish his food or tell her it was a good meal. My stomach growls as she scrapes the food from his plate into the trash.

He doesn't eat leftovers.

"You'd better not be eating that," he says, coming in to get the last of the wine.

Corrin smiles. "Oh, no," she says, rinsing the plate and putting it in the dishwasher. "I've had more than enough."

She wipes down the counters and starts the dishwasher, but she cleans the cast iron by hand.

~~7 PM – Clean the kitchen~~

Sounds from the game filter into the hall, the speakers poorly filtering the audio. Aiden is watching his favorite team while Corrin checks his outfits for the next day.

A good one for golf, paired with the shoes she polished today, and business casual for the office.

I doubt he's going to wear it, but he'd be stupid not to.

Anything he picks for himself is from a few seasons ago. While the clothes are new, his style is questionable.

Further proof that money can't buy taste.

~~8 PM – Prep Aiden's clothes for the next day~~

She does a full shower, hair, and makeup routine before bed, which is purely for his benefit. The kind of natural makeup look that takes a minimum of ten products and years of skill to perfect.

The lingerie she's wearing matches her floral dressing robe.

She's gorgeous.

~~9 PM – Shower and makeup~~

Aiden comes in, dressed so sloppily he resembles a rumpled t-shirt that was stuffed between the couch cushions. It's not an attractive look, especially compared to the level of effort Corrin has invested.

The way she presents herself makes it clear that while he isn't violent, this isn't consensual, either. She's fulfilling an obligation, but he doesn't give a shit about how she's feeling. He thrusts into her like she's a hole in the mattress and rolls off of her with a satisfied grunt. She lies there staring at the ceiling.

She doesn't move.

He doesn't put his arms around her, but brushes a rough kiss against her forehead, turns over, and closes his eyes.

~~10 PM – Sex, lounge with Aiden 'til he sleeps~~

Once he's snoring, she slips out of bed and goes back into the bathroom. The light goes on, and she's in there for a while. When she gets back into bed, her makeup has been replaced with night cream.

She turns off the lamp on her nightstand.

~~11 PM – Take off makeup and go to sleep~~

The recycling goes out on Tuesday, and the trash goes out on Thursday. The housekeeper usually comes on Monday, Wednesday, and Friday. Saturday and Sunday schedules are up in the air since Aiden makes all their social plans.

It looks like this week is going to be a little different. There's a note on the calendar that the housekeeper is going to be there on Thursday instead of Wednesday.

I think she could be Corrin's alibi, and since I'm pretty sure the woman has been sneaking Corrin birth control, I want to make sure they're both in the clear.

I type a note to myself so I don't forget.

Reminder: Housekeeper coming THURSDAY

FIVE

From what I've seen, Aiden does the same thing every day. The office space he keeps is purely for optics. He doesn't do much work there, but he doesn't have to.

After his perfectly orchestrated morning, he spends four to six hours in meetings that usually include lunch and golf. After that, he may spend some time at the office, but usually he stays at the course.

As far as following him, the social club is out, but I know how long I have to prepare once he's there. He's pretty good at golf, so if he heads to the green, I know I have around five hours.

I use the time to take care of myself.

For this job, my ID says I'm Clair Bowin, and Clair has a week pass to the local Fit Shack. Their only camera is pointed at the front entrance. I pull the ball cap down over my face and trip through the door so it gets a good clean shot of the top of my head.

It's worth the trouble for the hot shower, and the prepaid Visa doesn't draw any undue attention. I exfoliate, shave my legs, and detangle my curls in the shower.

It's not everyday I get to pamper myself.

I'd planned to work on this for at least two weeks, but I don't think Corrin has much time before Aiden starts to get agitated again. Last time, he lost his shit over a missing receipt.

I try not to think of all the people I'm not getting to in time. I know I can't be everywhere at once, but it still keeps me awake some nights, especially knowing my mother was one of these women.

I get back before Corrin goes out for her run. And it's so late, I have to double-check the time. Even if she does half her usual route, about five miles winding through the neighborhood, she'll be late to start dinner.

I can't tell if she miscalculated her run or not.

Maybe she thought she would have more time after the last beating and apology cycle. But judging from the discoloration I've seen, it's been three days. Her bruises from last time haven't yet faded to the purple and yellow they get when they're starting to heal.

I already know dinner will be late, and I'm sure there's something else I haven't thought of yet. This isn't going to be her usual schedule.

From what I've seen, there are two things Aiden is worried about most of all. The way he looks (by extension, how his wife makes him look) and money.

She's still running when he pulls into the driveway, and I switch to their home security feed as he backs into the four-car garage next to her old silver model luxury car.

There's a yellow coat of pollen on his black one. He traces a finger through it and mutters something under his breath. If I had to guess, I'd say Aiden had another rough day at the golf course. The garage door is already closing, leaving him in a dim gray shadow that warms as he flips on the lights by the back door.

She hasn't greeted him. The recycling is still out by the road, and there's no drink in his hand.

Even on the grainy image from the camera, I can see his jaw tense. It's eerie watching the windup, knowing Corrin is running home.

He takes a beer out of the fridge, then reaches for a chilled glass instead of his usual whisky cocktail. He presses the power button on the TV remote but leaves the volume turned down low. He paces a circuit from his office at the end of the hall to the foyer.

Just watching his aimless wandering makes me anxious, and a pit forms in my stomach. A well-placed security camera picks up an overhead view of his movements, but I can't see his expression when he reaches the door at the end of the hallway, looking through the glass pane for any sign of his wife.

I watch from the window of my van as she finishes the final leg of her aborted run. She's at least forty-five minutes behind schedule.

This couldn't have happened at a worse time.

SIX

Aiden opens the door and moves back making space for Corrin as she walks up the paving stones to the front entrance of the house.

I am too far away to tell if it is tension in her shoulder or perfect posture, but her pace slows before she steps onto the patio. She glances around furtively for any witnesses, then walks past him into their foyer.

He closes the door behind her.

I focus on their home security camera feed and shift in my seat, pulling on my headphones and adjusting the volume so I can hear them both clearly.

"I thought you were running today. At two." His hand grips her thin wrist. "This afternoon."

She goes still.

"Yes, I meant to." Her voice is quiet, and her head is bowed a little as she speaks. I can't see her face, but her shoulders seem to dip in towards each other as if she is withering.

He lifts her chin with his index finger. "Look at me." The words are soft, cold, and commanding.

The hair on the back of my arms stands on end. My gut already tightening in anticipation of what is about to happen.

His fingers creep up to grasp her jaw, his face so close to hers that his words don't reach the microphone.

She looks more like a frightened rabbit than the confident woman she had been just a few minutes ago.

He doesn't let her pull away from him as he shouts into her face. "Then what were you doing today?"

"I'm sorry, I'm sorry, I'm sorry," she starts chanting like she isn't aware of what he was asking, "I had to go back to the store. They gave me the wrong receipt. They had to reprint it. I'm sorry."

He hits her, his fist drawing back beside his own ribcage and striking her just below her sternum, his other hand still gripping her jaw, keeping her from sinking to the slick marble. He strikes her again in the same place, then lets go, stepping over her as she falls to the floor.

Just hold on, sweet girl.

He walks so calmly for a man who is actively terrorizing his wife, carefully picking through the receipts in the gold tray by the front door.

He reads them over once, then starts again.

"So where the fuck were you between one and four this afternoon?"

Silence.

Say something, Corrin. Come on. Push through it.

He stalks back toward where she's curled on the cold tile.

"Answer me!"

He kicks her viciously, striking her in the breasts and stomach.

I breathe deeply, like I can somehow fill both of our lungs, not allowing myself to turn my back. I owe her. Someone has to witness it, see her, know exactly what he does and why he deserves what is coming to him. I let her pain into my soul, let her fear pass into me. As if he won't damage her quite as much as long as I am watching—if I don't look away, it won't hurt her.

Because sorrow shared is sorrow halved.

It frightens me how quiet she is, but I keep taking slow inhales and exhales like the extra oxygen in my lungs can somehow go to her.

Part of me hopes she passes out, but I've seen enough crimes to know that blows like these take your breath away. The pain is so bad, it's as if someone is trying to vacuum seal your lungs shut.

She gags, her hands sliding out in front of her as she pulls herself across the floor, not going anywhere, just numbly trying to move away from the pain. Purely reflex.

"Where the fuck are you going to go?"

She doesn't answer.

Please stop. Just stay down.

As if I am here coaching in a boxing match she never signed up for.

He grabs the hair at the nape of her neck. For a moment, I think he might bash her face against the white marble tile in the foyer. But he wouldn't do that. He is far too vain to damage the face of one of his prize possessions. I am grateful for that.

I grit my teeth as he rips her clothes off.

The elastic of her yoga pants seems to fight him as he pulls up her sports bra. He leans his face in close, examining her skin. He bends like he's going to sniff her, leaving her bare breasts pinned awkwardly under the band before working her pants down her thighs.

This is not part of the routine.

I didn't want to see this. This is too much, and yet, I can't leave her alone with him. Even if I am only on the other side of a radio frequency she knows nothing about. I pull a tissue from the box on my desk and blot my cheeks dry, clenching my teeth together, and force my eyes to the screen. *I'm sorry, I'm sorry, I'm sorry.* I don't try to wipe away the fresh tears that run—I let them fall pouring all my sadness into a box I rename rage, watching as he shoves his hands into her underwear.

He rubs his fingers together.

As if she would ever cheat on him. She was already so terrified of missing a receipt, she risked going back for it.

There had never been an option that wouldn't lead her to this place, the cold tile on her cheeks and her husband bent over, beating and raping her for an easily explained mistake that could only be misconstrued by him as a means of finding fault with her.

My nails bite into the edge of the desk. I am hot and cold all at once. I can't help feel a little guilty, as if I am taking courage from her.

She doesn't cry or make any sound as he bunches her pants around her knees.

I'm grateful that his back is to the camera, blocking my view.

His movements are rushed and abrupt, her knees pushed up toward her chest as he moves sharply at first before he settles into a sweaty cadence.

The sounds of skin squeaking across marble, his panting, and grunting fill the headset. I lift the headphones from my ears, but keep my gaze on the screen. His movement stutters, then goes still.

He stands when he finishes, walking through the arched kitchen door to grab one of the floral-printed towels from the bar on the oven. He uses it to wipe himself off, then walks back to the foyer and tosses it at her face.

She doesn't move, and there is a moment when a chill runs up my spine even though I know she isn't dead. Maybe he feels it, too, because he prods her with his foot.

She moans.

Pain. Good. Pain is good. It means you're still alive.

He smoothes his rumpled shirt before tucking it in and zipping his pants. "Now clean this shit up and get some dinner on the fucking table. I'm starving."

SEVEN

The next morning, Corrin leaves the house at *8:00*. I track her car to the neighborhood's gate, then change feeds to check on Aiden.

His webcam on his work computer shows he's sitting at his desk looking intently at something. He hasn't noticed the little light that indicates the built-in camera is on and has been on for a week.

At *8:15*, I shut down their home security cameras. I won't need the video feed from the house, but I watch the one from his office 'til he notices the blanks where the view of his home should be.

With traffic like this, it should take him at least ten minutes to get home. That means within the next five minutes, I need to be inside to be sure I have everything in place before he arrives.

I have two and a half hours to get in, complete the kill and get out.

At the front door, I press the number combination that I know by heart. Aiden isn't that creative—*GOLF* spelled out in numbers: 4-6-5-3 and *LOVER*: 5-6-8-3-7. Not to worry. When he uses it on his work computer, he uses actual letters and adds his birthday: 0-4-0-5 and an exclamation mark because symbols are required.

If I gave a damn, I'd check to see if he uses that on everything, but I'm out of time.

No.

Corrin is out of time. Soon, if left unattended, he will kill her.

The door beeps when it unlocks, but everything else in the house is silent. That's a good thing. It means the electronics are off, just how I left them.

My shoe covers glide across the floor. The hair net fits comfortably over my wig.

I run the razor wire across the entrance and make my way down the hall to his man cave. Funny how every inch of the house is covered with cameras, but not this one room. He protects his privacy. Or, he thinks he does.

I don't want anything in here, but I know how to make it look good—messy, confusing, amateur. Taking some of the things that look valuable, but aren't, I set them aside. As if I meant to take them with me. I move the external hard drives out in plain view so they will be sure to check them, and notice if someone was looking for specific information. Leaving cash in an obvious place is the second-to-last step.

I remove the front case from his desktop and, after shutting it down, pull the hard drive. Or I start to. I hear him at the front door, I lower my mask to be sure he can tell I'm a woman.

He's the kind of guy who will see my face and it will make him overly confident. I paste on a placid expression and step toward the entrance so he will see me as soon as he walks inside.

I bend my knees a little, ready to move, and stand in the threshold to wait.

"Hey, handsome," I say as the door swings open.

He freezes, and I can't stop the grin that spreads over my face.

He doesn't notice the wire strung across the doorway or the box cutter in my hand. It's like that prank where people string clear tape or cling wrap across doorways, waiting for someone to walk into it.

He charges.

When I don't move, he looks surprised. His head snaps up as he sees the dark line of wire, and his hands reach for it like he might be able to stop himself, but even if he does, I'm ready for him.

I don't always like to play with my food, but…

There's something special about Corrin. Don't get me wrong, they're all important. But with her, there's something extra about how good she is. *Kind* to him. And for herself, the one thing she can't do is leave. I know if she tried, he would kill her for sure.

I press the button to open the box cutter just as Aiden runs into the wire.

Red mist sprays across the white walls and marble. I've heard it's really difficult to get out of marble. Blood, that is. I don't know. I've never tried.

He's gagging when he hits the floor, his hands grasping at his neck to staunch the bleeding. His eyes are wide. He's frightened. Good. The adrenaline will kick in, and he'll have a burst of energy and power. I haven't cut anything too important. He'd be still already if it had. That's fine, though. I want the time to talk to him.

"I've always wondered how it feels to have a cut like that. How long it will take you to die. I have to admit, I've never used this method. I mean, I've killed before. Lots of times. But not like this." I bend closer, waiting for a response. "Does it hurt? Can you talk?"

He doesn't say anything.

"I've been working so much, I've hardly had the chance to talk to anyone. It's okay if you can't. I don't want you to strain yourself."

There's a moment when I can see the sclera around his eyes.

The wound isn't going to kill him right away. It is going to hurt like hell. He might not be able to talk again, but if I don't finish him off, he'll live.

"That is marvelous!" I laugh. "Really, I had no idea if this would work. Like I said, I don't usually do this, but I've been so bored, I was dying to try something new. Well, not *dying*."

This time my laugh is genuine.

"Not in the same way you're going to, but I was really eager to try this. Like, so excited you don't even know. I'm sorry. I must seem like a total nerd. I haven't let you get a word out."

I stop.

"Do you think this is how Corrin was feeling the other day, when you raped her on the kitchen floor?" I ask, growing serious again, and I can feel the tears pricking at my eyes.

"Ugh, I'm sorry," I say, wiping my face with the back of my sleeve. "It's just that it was really hard to watch what you did to her. You know, I've seen your old wedding website with all the pictures. And honestly? I'm sorry you can't talk because I would genuinely like to know what happened. When—*why*—you decided it was okay to treat her like that."

I squat down on the balls of my feet and really look into his eyes. "What do you think Corrin would say if she found you like this?"

"Oh," I clap a hand over my mouth to hide my laugh when I see the dark spot spread across his khaki pants. "Don't be embarrassed. That happens a lot in situations like this. Dying is so messy. I know disorder is not really your thing, but given the special circumstances, I think you'll learn to make your peace with it."

I look at my watch.

8:47

"Look at that. We have plenty of time. In the future, I'll have to remember that 'not-being-able-to-talk' thing. That really is a bummer."

He glances up at the camera and gives his best attempt at a smile.

"Ah, yes, that's not going to help you. I already took care of the video feed. I did, however, leave that bit of footage—what you did—for investigators to find. I think someone should know."

There's a hopeful glimmer in his eyes at the mention. Perhaps, the idea of his wife. Like he thinks, despite everything he's done to her, she might do something to save him. And he's right. She probably would, but only out of fear or terror—of what could happen if she didn't, and he lived, anyway. The cost to her would be immeasurable. He would make bail and kill her if it was the last thing he did.

I won't be letting that happen.

EIGHT

I look at my watch again. Time seems to be crawling by.

8:51

"She won't be home for a few hours. Do you think she'll feel better or worse if she's the one to find your body? I've been wondering about it because on the one hand, seeing a dead body? Traumatic. And I would know. Especially when it's someone you love. But I can't figure out if she still loves you. I'm sure she would love to be free. I know she wants you to stop hitting her. But there's a big difference between wishing someone was dead and wanting them to stop hurting you. You know? Well, I guess you don't." I say with a wry smile.

"Anyway, I decided for her, because whether she knows it—actually, you might not know this either—you will eventually kill her. Even if you don't mean to. That sucks, doesn't it? You'll probably swear, or you would if you could talk, that you would never hurt her—or you'll never do it again, but that's why I watch you for a while first, I know this wasn't a one-off. You do this a lot. It's kinda like a serial killer. You always escalate. I know, you probably think, 'Well, if it isn't the pot calling the kettle,' but there aren't a lot of studies about people like me. We don't tend to get caught." I smile.

"But you—there are loads of studies about men like you. And, statistically speaking, you don't stop. You're like rabid animals. There isn't a cure. They have to be put down, which, in their case, is always very sad. But you?" I shrug. "I really don't give a shit. Because you had a choice. You've had a hundred opportunities to stop. But you haven't, have you?"

I look at my watch again.

8:53

"Well, Aiden, this has been a blast, but what do you say we cut things short?" I lift my hand and show him the box cutter. "I know it will cause her some trauma, but you have good life insurance. She'll be able to afford therapy, and I think overall Corrin will sleep better at night knowing you're in the dirt and it's not a trick. I think she'll want to know that you can't follow her or hunt her down because she'll be the one to find your body, check your pulse, and know beyond a doubt that you are dead. I've thought about it, and it just feels *right* to me."

When I stand and step toward him, he scrambles back away from me, slipping and sliding in a crab walk. The front of his shirt is stained with blood, and more slides down his neck where his hand had applied pressure. His boat shoes leave streaks of blood and urine on the marble floor, though his pants absorb most of it.

"Any last words?" I ask. "I know you can't talk, but I can give you some time to write something in blood. You've got a good bit on your hands." I smirk. "I'd probably write on the wall. It tends to smear on marble, plus, you don't want to smudge it with your death rattle and all." I smile encouragingly. "You can say whatever you want. Don't worry, I'm not going to clean it up when you're dead."

His hand trembles as he lifts it toward the white wall. It's funny how he's gotten so much more comfortable making messes now that he knows he isn't going to make it out of here. He starts to write.

BLACK, BLONDE WOMAN, WORE A WHITE PAINTER'S SUIT TURNED OFF

He can't reach further than that before he runs out of wall.

"You know, Aiden, I'm not a natural blonde. A look at my brows would have told you that, but this is a pretty good wig. It's made with real human hair." I wiggle my eyebrows playfully. "Now, let's get down to business. This is my favorite part."

He really tries to scream this time, his ruined vocal cords flapping uselessly, visible through the gaping wound over his trachea.

I'm surprised he's still breathing.

The human body really is amazing.

When I take his hand, he tries to pull away, kicking pathetically like a child who doesn't want to go to school, but I take a firm grip and pull his bare wrist toward me then drag the knife up his arm along the inside of his wrist while I explain my thought process. "See, if I cut across, the veins will actually pull up into the arm and slow the bleeding. That's actually quite survivable. You know the saying, 'Across is for attention, but the long way's for results.' Or something like that. It's really a pretty tacky thing to say, but you get the point. And the carotid or jugular are too quick. Plus, there's more splatter."

I cut deep, watching the blood flow in silence for a moment. Then reach for his other arm.

He doesn't fight me this time. He's getting weaker.

The blood that comes is more than a trickle and pools on the floor, pulsing with his slowing heartbeat.

I stand back to watch him, observing to make sure the bleeding lessens. I always wait 'til it stops before I check for a pulse. Dead bodies don't bleed.

When he isn't moving anymore, I glance at my watch again.

9:07

The bleeding has stopped. I lean down and press my gloved fingers to the right side of his neck. Blood oozes from the wound across his throat when I touch him, but there's no pulse.

There's always a weight in my stomach when I finish a job.

A little sadness.

At one time, however long ago, he was a beautiful baby with a bright future ahead of him.

But this was the path he chose.

I picture what he did to Corrin, and the hollow place in my stomach releases.

Killing Aiden was the right thing to do. It was the only way of setting Corrin free.

I did the right thing.

He earned this.

I'm still a good person.

I think about other executioners and how they get some form of plausible deniability. Two people at the switches for the electric chair, someone firing blanks with a firing squad, lethal injection being a team effort and applied by a machine. They get to take the easy way out. Isn't that just about the state of the world?

Women always have to do the hard work, the dirty work. It takes us a lot of extra steps just to get justice.

I feel a little guilty leaving such a big mess for Corrin and the maid. Maybe she'll call in a crime scene cleaning crew. I hope so.

I step back, swapping out my shoe covers, putting the old ones into the black trash bag from my pocket. I take off the outer painters suit and put that in the black trash bag along with the first set of gloves.

I keep the second set of latex gloves on over the steel mesh ones that protect my hands, just in case the box cutter were to slip.

When I've finished that little bit of cleanup, I double-check myself for any obvious signs of splatter.

I open the garage and sling the bag into the trash, then roll the can out to the curb.

9:15

Just in time. The rattle and bang of the garbage truck sounds at the entrance of the subdivision.

I grab the antenna for the mesh network I set up from the underside of the mailbox and walk to my van. I take off the last set of shoe covers before I get in and drive toward the interstate.

It's time to get out of Alabama.

ABBY

NINE

I stop by a small bookstore and get something new to read for this forced vacation. It's about a girl who falls down a magical well and makes friends with a talking mouse. A perfect distraction.

I head toward the beach near Tybee Island on the South Carolina side. It's one of the busy tourist traps with cameras everywhere, but a little place off the beaten path. While not technically a public beach, there are other cars and vans parked along the roads here. And since I mind my own business, nobody will bother me.

The road turns sandy and ends with a beautiful tree-lined view.

As soon as I park, I swap out my boots for flip-flops, change my black pants to shorts, and head down the lane to the beach. It's a short hike, and I arrive just in time to see the sunset.

This place makes me think about Mom. It makes me wonder if the good memory I felt so drawn to was a lie. She brought me here for a sun-filled day of laughter. In my memory, she glows, radiantly happy. But now, the picture in my mind's eye seems shrouded in a foggy gray cloud. I sit beyond the reach of the water's cold grasp and run my fingers through the sand.

Had I erased the sadness in her eyes with my childish wonder and replaced it with my excitement for a beach day? It is difficult to say. Mostly because I can't always place things in time. Was this days or weeks before she died? I don't even know if it's real. Were we already on the run? I'm not sure of any of it, and now the whole golden memory feels like a lie.

Or maybe a dream.

A grim overlay of how things happened, how I remember them happening, cycles over the memory like walking between a projector and a movie screen. This place isn't the way I remembered it.

It feels colder.

It felt like I was in the house for days before Percilla came and took me away.

I had wet my pants. I think they were real underwear with soft pink hearts on them. Mom was excited for me to be potty-trained, so she got me the expensive ones. It was going to be big for the budget, not having to buy diapers anymore.

A tear slides down my cheek.

This memory feels real. That joy—that was real.

I was helping her. Our family of two was a team.

We were going to start our own life. Maybe we already had in that two-bedroom house on the quiet, tree-lined street.

She died there. That much is true. Red blood seeping into the floor, the power shut off, and me hiding in the closet by the door with the winter coats piled on top of me. It was so hot I could hardly breathe.

"Be still and quiet for mamma, okay, baby?"

She said that to me, and I was good. I was quiet—even when my father came in and I could hear her crying.

I know what it sounds like when someone beats another person to death, when one human pleads with another for their life. I've had people beg me before, too, and it's different. Because I've heard someone ask them for pity. But no one showed my mother mercy.

Knowing his daughter was due home from school, he still beat the mother of his child, shot her, and left her to die.

I wonder if she could hear me, begging her to wake up. Did that make it worse? Dying like that, knowing she was leaving me alone?

Or was she already so far gone it didn't break through all the pain?

I rub the tears from my face when I realize I'm no longer alone on the beach. This is my pain, and I don't have to share it with anybody.

This is why I hate vacations. Too much time to think.

The breeze smells of salt, and I turn my face toward the horizon.

I can't help feeling resentment towards the people who are here to enjoy the beautiful sunset. Couples holding hands, walking along the water's edge.

And I'm curious about the man standing alone in the shadow of a tree looking out over the dunes toward the sea. I wonder if sorrow threatens to swallow him the same way it's started to overwhelm me.

He glances my way, his attention drawn by my staring.

I nod and look away, walking quickly back up the road towards where I parked my van.

Although his face is covered by the shade of the trees, I can see he is tall and lean with broad shoulders.

As I get closer to him, he drops his DSLR camera into a black backpack and slings the bag over his shoulder.

Something tells me we're not here for the same reason.

I don't sleep well when I'm not working, but I try to catch up on activity the way I can't when I'm on a job. My active hobbies are things I can do solo and without much equipment. Running, climbing, swimming. Calisthenics are nice, especially since there are parks with workout equipment, places I can go and not have to talk to people, where cameras are few—if they exist or work at all.

So I burn as much of my free time as I can on exercise and training for the next job. I can also study coming industry changes. Plus I need time to stay as up to speed as I can on cybersecurity and the newest smart home gadgets coming out.

It's one of the reasons it's important to know what skills a person has before starting a new job. As much as I'd like to help people, there are just some skill sets I can't go up against. At least, not on their home turf. But most people have to leave their houses at least once a week. Still, this time off isn't just a break.

I can tell when Percilla is trying to keep me away from something.

And so far, there are only two places she's done that—Virginia and the Midwest.

I have a look about me that isn't common in the wilderness of the Midwest. And if I were to get in trouble, her network hasn't expanded enough in the area to help.

I've been to the East Coast and worked in other parts of Virginia, but she's kept me away from the estates and farmland.

I know she has resources at play in Thomas Jefferson's home state, but I'm just not one of them. Or, I haven't been. And now I know why. I suspect that I'm from somewhere between here and Virginia.

The primary location, Mother Mercy Mission, is on the outskirts of a very accessible city. From time to time, Percilla sends me to one of the satellite locations, and one of the women will bring me supplies.

There's usually an expression of pity. They think I'm running, one of those *#vanlife* girlies who's had a rough time with an ex. Who could blame them after some of the stories a few years back?

Even with all the surveillance and a lot of circumstantial evidence, we can all think of a few names of men who've gotten away with murder. Allegedly.

I know Percilla will say it's too soon for me to go back to work. Corrin is still in the news. They identified her without having to actually say her name. "Widow of Aiden Lancaster the Third returned home to find her husband…"

They did show her picture, though. She looked shaken, but not sad. The housekeeper was with her when she got home. They arrived at the same time. Fortunately, the maid service employee was very familiar with the household and verified that Mrs. Lancaster had a consistent routine.

Not one fucking question about the bruises on her neck.

I don't want to hear anymore of it.

I'm glad she's safe, but knowing anything else about that dead prick will have me wanting to dig his ass up and kill him all over again.

After five days near the beach and a second sighting of the tall, thin man, it's time to move to a new spot and finish my vacation.

It's never a good thing to become a regular somewhere.

Percilla and I haven't spoken about our fight again or the things she's not willing to tell me, like who my father is or the name of the town where I was born. I figure that's why she hasn't asked how much I remember. Not because she couldn't handle hearing about it or because she doesn't care, but because if she did ask, we'd have to actually talk. She'd have to be honest with me. I know my father is a killer, but I'm pretty sure I've dealt with worse. She'll have to give me something that I should actually be afraid of before I give up on finding out the truth.

Sometimes I forget she's old enough that she could be my grandmother. Not that sixty-one is old. But it's easy to forget that she's seen things and in some ways knows more about me than I do myself. There's a chance she knows my family or has seen them. I can't help but wonder if she plans to take my history to her grave.

I could always go and see her.

Would it be this easy for her to keep her secrets if she had to refuse me to my face?

I call her from South Carolina.

I'm relieved when she doesn't answer.

When I stop for the night, I make myself wait 'til after dinner before I open my laptop and pull up the scanned newspaper clipping. I read through it slowly, looking for any details I might have missed the first time. But there are no dates on the story, no exact locations in the article, and the clipping seems to be from the middle of the page. I can't even tell what paper it's from or who wrote the article.

Everything I search is coming up blank.

Turns out, there are a lot of Judge Jackson's. Not just in the country, but also specifically in Virginia. None of them match.

The family of Tara Jackson, a Virginia woman found beaten and shot to death in her Georgia home, has been exhumed and moved back to her hometown for reburial.

The family is still searching for answers about her missing daughter, Mara. There have been no leads in this cold case in twenty years. Mara went missing the day her mother was murdered and hasn't been seen since.

The move comes after the death of Judge Vernon Jackson, father-in-law of Tara and grandfather of Mara. Judge Jackson is survived by his sons, Police Chief Bill Jackson, Commonwealth's Attorney Tom Jackson, and grandson Roland Jackson.

The family has released the following statement:

"We are grateful to be bringing our beloved Tara home. We are still searching for our Mara, but we are confident that we will find her and bring her home."

I'm even closer to Virginia now, and I'm not working. The temptation is strong, but I shouldn't head there yet.

Not until I have a plan.

Not until I know exactly where I'm going, what I want to say, and who I want to say it to. I don't want to stumble into town like an idiot and spook the people I'm looking for.

I've picked this fight with Percilla, but I know I'm not going back for family. Even if there are cousins looking for me, I don't need them. I have Percilla.

My motive is a meld of morbid curiosity and a need to get the same justice for myself that I get for the victims I help. I wonder if she would be more understanding if I just told her that.

I don't think I can tell her.

Maybe Percilla has already guessed.

Somehow, it's just easier to bring up the same argument from a different angle and hope that she'll trust me to figure it out for myself.

She's seen me handle people who want to kill their wives.

Mom isn't the only person who was abused, and she won't be the last. And there are things that are far worse than death.

If it were just that, I'm sure Percilla wouldn't put up so much resistance. But there's something else she's not telling me, and I have to find out what it is.

I get back on the road before sunrise to beat the morning rush.

TEN

I wait 'til I've made it to Georgia before I call in again.

Percilla sounds annoyed when she answers the phone. "Goddamn it! You let him write something? What if they had found you?"

"They weren't going to find me. I had at least two-and-a-half hours' head start, if not more. This guy was really anal about schedules and routines. How is the wife doing?"

"They still haven't said her name, but it's a big story, and everyone is speculating. I think you should consider taking some more time off."

I ignore the statement. I just came off a hiatus, and I'm not doing that again. For a while, at least. "Did they spot the van?"

"Yes." She pauses. "They're looking for a white van."

"They're always looking for a white van. I did a—"

"No," she cuts in. "Don't tell me what color the wrap is. Just—did you get it on there good?"

"Yes, and you worry too much."

"I don't know. Something just feels off. Someone's been looking up your mother. Called the shelter and everything."

"What? Who was it? Was it a man?"

"It was her old name, but I don't like it. It's been twenty years. Why are they looking now? They never gave a shit back when someone could have done something."

Sometimes it feels like she knows just how to distract me from our arguments. We're both quiet for a while, thinking about what it is that makes us do this kind of work. There's still the tension between us too. The one where she won't tell me what I want to know, and she's wondering if I found a way around her mandate. Neither of us wants to address it head-on. Not again.

I hate that we're awkward around each other right now.

"How is the shelter? Donations?"

"Good, it's been really positive. I think you were right about accepting the crypto and letting the victims you've served donate, too. We're going to be able to do a lot of good. Help a lot of people."

"That's good. I'm really glad."

"Are you okay?" she asks.

"Yes, it was a bad one. I don't know how much they're going to release on this, but it made me think more about Mom and the article."

We're both quiet again, this time for longer. Neither of us wants to give in, and neither of us wants to fight about it more. It's also odd that she's telling me any of this. Weird that the newspaper article comes out and someone calls the shelter looking for Mom. I'm just about to ask her when Percilla breaks the silence. "The next one might actually be worse."

"How bad?"

"I'm torn between thinking about how much you need a break and how long these two can hold on."

"Two?"

"There's a child."

"Fuck."

"Yeah," she says, and her tone tells me I can't possibly imagine.

"Is it the mom or the kid?"

"I think it's the girl. I'm not even sure if the mother knows. But the woman is mostly homebound."

"So, who wrote the letter?"

"The girl."

"Send it."

"Incoming."

I can hear her typing in the background.

"Just—if it's too much when you see it, if you need to take some time, for your mental health…"

She never asks what I remember outright, and when I've asked Percilla about her past, she never answers those questions either. I don't think she's told anyone her story, but maybe it's just me she refuses to talk to.

Parents aren't supposed to burden their children with their trauma. At least, that's what she says when I ask. But she seems to know a lot about how my mind works, even when I don't say all I'm feeling.

"I'll be okay," I tell her. "I can take it. I'm not leaving a kid like that. You didn't leave me."

"It was the only good thing I did then. You know that, right?"

"I'm glad you came back for me."

She's quiet when she says, "I should have saved your mom."

"Did he ever ask about me?" I ask, changing the subject. "My father?" I add, like there was anyone else.

"No," she says flatly.

I know that tone.

She's not going to talk about this. She always gets short with me, but knowing she just wants to keep me safe doesn't mean I'm going to stop bringing it up.

I can't seem to resist it when the answers are so close.

"I want to know where they moved her body."

"You already know more than you want to."

"I looked for her. Did you know that none of the records were digitized? When the courthouse burned, so did all the records. What if I have cousins or siblings? What if they're stuck, too? What if they need someone like me? People like us?"

"It's too dangerous. You think you want to go there, but you don't. I can promise you that."

"You can promise whatever you want, but I'm going to find out one way or another. The question is, are you going to be honest with me or not?"

"This is me being honest with you. If he finds you, he'll never let you walk away from him again. All of this will be over. And whomever you might have helped, whatever good you could have done in the world, those people will be on their own. And so will you."

"So if I keep looking, you're going to abandon me?" I scoff.

"Abby, you don't understand what you're dealing with."

"Then tell me what it is I should be so afraid of!"

"I didn't realize I'd raised such a selfish child." She says it softly, almost like she doesn't realize I can still hear her. "He has a place in Virginia. Or, at least, he used to. His grandfather was a judge, his father was the district attorney, and his uncle was the chief of police."

"I know that. I can read. Tell me something that's not in the paper. Tell me where."

"Orange, I think."

"What was his name?" I ask, recognizing it as the town where the courthouse was.

"That depended on the day."

"When was he there?"

"Abby," she pleads.

"When was it?"

She's silent.

"I didn't realize I was raised by such a selfish woman," I say, feeling a cold rage build in me.

"If you need to think that, it's fine. I've survived worse."

Guilt washes over me, and an apology lodges like a lump in my throat. "Percilla," I begin, but she cuts me off.

"Goodnight, Abby. I love you." Then she hangs up.

"I love you, too," I say, even though I know she's already gone.

OLIVIA

Dear Mother,

I have a mother already, but that's just what Mrs. Martin says I should call you. She is good. She's helping me write this. She just can't help me anymore because mom's new husband won't let her.

This is my last chance. If you can't help me, I don't think anyone can.

Mrs. Martin says that's not how step dads are supposed to be. I wish I could talk to her more because she always understands. It's not that momma doesn't understand, or wouldn't, it's just that I haven't told her. She's been so sick and Eddy has been really good to her. They've even decided to get married so she could be on his insurance.

I feel so guilty for it. I do want her to have good things, nice things, and if I could just stick it out, I know it would help her a lot. I never liked him, he was always weird, but after we moved in with him he got worse.

He started coming to my room to "say goodnight." My room is upstairs over the living room, next to his office.

Mom can't do stairs. She gets too dizzy and sometimes, she passes out.

At first, he did just say goodnight, but then he started being weird. He asked me to get ready for bed, like get my PJs on and stuff like that. I don't like to write about it, I told Mrs. Martin some, what I was comfortable saying. She never asks me to say more than I'm comfortable with.

She said that I should tell momma, but I feel like that wouldn't be right. What if she asked him about it and he hurt her for it? What if she doesn't believe me or I got in trouble like he says I will if I tell anyone?

I'm so scared. Please help me.

Olivia

ELEVEN

When I'm finished reading the dossier, I get out of the van and throw up in the bushes. I heave and retch 'til my stomach is empty, then I rinse my mouth out with water and brush my teeth.

I get back in the van and take I75 to I40, heading to middle Tennessee. Lobelville is little more than a pimple on God's ass crack in the Bible Belt.

Legend says the trees were sprayed with Agent Orange to help with the primary trade, or the primary legal trade. They don't have a lot, but what they do have, they've got plenty of. Logging, cancer, unemployment, and meth, but not specifically in that order.

The main challenge here is that since it's such a small town, everyone knows each other.

A stranger sticks out like a rainbow at a goth convention.

I swap out the navy blue wrap on the van for a simple black. It looks more official. People might be a bit suspicious of me, but that's not a problem. Because everything is so far apart, I can be sure of a slow response from the cops. Plus, nobody wants to talk to the police because, "Fuck 'em." Also, meth.

I don't always luck out, but the house next door is for sale. They've moved to the big city, Dixson. The only way someone will be out here is if they're looking to buy. I can plan for that.

Though I doubt anybody is interested in six acres so full of junked cars, it looks like a wrecking yard.

I stop on the side of the road before I get to the driveway and set a trail cam, then move my van to the back of the property, behind most of the vehicles, where the neighbors can't see.

The house where Olivia lives is just on the other side of the tree line. A two-story farmhouse style with a shiny new tin roof and a paved drive that must have cost a small fortune. The bus stop is just over a half-mile away, by the main road. There are multiple houses down this gravel road. And the kids wait for it in the telltale shack by the wooden rail of mailboxes. That's before the split. Three on the left branch, three on the right.

The main drag, Highway 13, is at least five miles and several turns away, and they'd still have to figure out if it should be the Linden or Lobelville police department reporting.

My lucky day.

I check the local paper to see if there's any news that might change my approach. I find a couple of old issues, and one announces that Edward Draper married Samantha Jones at the hill chapel on a Sunday. They were closed for church services on Saturday.

Olivia was telling the truth.

Day one is the usual. I get my bearings and spend most of the afternoon doing surveillance. Since I'm in the backwoods, I watch through binoculars from the front seat of the van.

I make a rough schedule for Olivia so I can track it and see if this is what she does every day.

```
6:00 AM Wake up
6:15 AM Get ready for school
7:00 AM Bike to the bus stop
7:30 AM Bus ride to school
8:00 AM–3:15 PM At school
3:20 PM Bus pickup
```

```
3:50 PM Bike home from bus stop
4:00 PM Homework
6:30 PM Free time
7:00 PM Dinner
8:15 PM Get ready for bed
```

I don't see any way around it. I'm going to have to place a mic while Samantha is home. It's risky, but I'm almost confident if I do it just after Olivia goes to school and Eddy has left for work, I can get in and out before she sees me. But I don't actually know her limitations. I understand she uses a wheelchair, but it's not clear how much she needs it. In her letter, Olivia said that she doesn't do well with stairs, so if I can make it up there silently, placing the mic is a piece of cake.

Throughout the day, while Eddy and Olivia are out, I catch glimpses of the woman. Every so often, she wheels past a window, but I only see her cross the kitchen twice to reach the bathroom.

Not long after Olivia goes to bed, I see Eddy go upstairs each night, then he comes down again. It is difficult to fully make sense of what I'm seeing. It is clearly inappropriate, but I need to know specifics. It's essential to make the punishment match the crime.

There are two things I need to do to make this happen. One, the audio feed. Two, a time when my work will be uninterrupted.

I wait 'til day five, when I am fairly certain of Samantha's routine, before I sneak into the house to plant the mic on the light in Olivia's bedroom. I wait until she's in the bathroom, which gives me about twenty minutes. It usually takes her about thirty minutes in total. That leaves me five to get into the house once I'm sure she's settled in the bathroom, and five to get well away before she comes out. Ten minutes to plant the mic isn't bad, but with the high A-frame ceiling and no ladder, I'm going to be cutting it close.

I don't have time to properly search the house for a calendar or schedule right now, but I can always try again.

I still have several days of surveillance left before I act.

TWELVE

The house is old, elevated on a bricked-in foundation. The front porch and its swinging bench are nearly half a story up, providing protection from the creek that crosses the drive and winds back to a field that at one time was a pasture. There are several barns and outbuildings, all in the arduous process of decaying, stacked full of stored antique tools and ghostly equipment.

They speak of bygone times and people long forgotten. It may be a consequence of the land's forlorn features or a side effect of the nostrum of the town, but there is an unmistakable pall over the place. The kind that hangs over a person at the mere suggestion of visiting and brings a piercing joy upon leaving.

Darkness here is more intense than anywhere else. Still dampened by the pollution of industrial lights, but here, everything is more. The emptiness more vast, the silence more complete, and the isolation more bitter. In the city, everyone is alone, but here, even in a place where everyone knows each other, the physical separation is so isolating that a walk to the mailbox can leave you a half mile from the nearest soul.

It is eerie, and I don't like it. Even watching Olivia through the window, I can see the loneliness swimming around her.

She is folding laundry on the full bed. The bare bulb is bolted to the angled ceiling above her head. It's where I planted the mic.

The bed is laid directly on the painted hardwood floors. The same chocolate color that covers the floors also goes halfway up the wood-paneled walls to meet the faded avocado green wallpaper with its speckle of pink and white daisies. It is hard to tell the color of the ceiling in the wan yellow light, but I imagine it desperately wants to be white.

If I had to guess, I'd say the room either smells of damp, mothballs, or stale cigarettes, but that is merely based on the sorry state of the architecture.

Olivia is right about the timing, too.

He hasn't missed a night.

I can see her stepfather when he reaches the top of the stairs, a sallow-looking man with a scraggly salt and pepper beard. His wiry hair makes his head look larger than it actually is.

His paunch, by comparison, seems understated and disproportionately small, almost like he has swallowed a cantaloupe and half is lodged in his stomach.

Her door is open—no, there isn't a door on the hinges—and I can't help thinking that was an often-repeated instruction. "It's my house. And in this house, we keep the doors open." Then the door was removed altogether, bare brass still bolted to the frame.

Families don't keep secrets.

But families *do* keep secrets. I would know.

She wraps her arms tightly around her stomach.

A chill runs down my spine—sympathetic fear and disgust.

His voice is clear as he steps closer to her.

Nearer to the bug I placed.

Pops of static fill in the space between his words, but I can hear clearly as he says, "Time to get ready for bed."

I've seen him in her room the past few nights, but it's different when I can hear their voices.

She turns her back to him when she pulls off her T-shirt, and I understand that the charade of the past half hour has mostly consisted of placing her clothes in a way that allows her to turn her back to him as she reaches for her pajamas—blue and white tank top and shorts. A matching set.

"Turn this way," he says, his hand touching the bare flesh above her hip.

I can see the flinch from half a mile away.

She turns.

"No, take the bra off. It's not good to sleep in them. That will give you cancer."

I gag. I hate seeing this. I don't want her to be in there alone, and my usually distant presence doesn't feel appropriate. My skin flashes cold, and I grip the edge of my desk.

She turns to face him, her arm twisting behind her back so she can thumb open the hook and eye on her training bra.

She steps back again, narrowly missing his reach. "I don't like it."

"You don't like what?" he asks, his eyes not focused on her face.

Olivia looks like she might cry, but she blinks hard and arranges her face in a neutral expression. "I don't want you to touch me." Her small voice is quiet but clear.

"Both you and your mother are mine. You live in my house, I take care of my family, and it is my job to teach my household. To make sure you are ready to be a proper wife. It is your duty to submit and be a good daughter."

Run. But I know, she can't. She has no place to go.

"Take off your underwear."

Her panties are pink with little green hearts on them.

Someone is sobbing. I lift the ear cushion away from my ear and realize it's me. But even if it breaks me, I will stay with her. I open an airplane bottle of vodka and take a shot to steel my nerves. I fight the temptation to grab my knife and go in now. There would be no possibility of a clean getaway.

Both Olivia and Samantha would see me, maybe even fight me, not knowing who I am or why I'm there.

I think of the hundred other girls just like Olivia, victims I won't be able to help if I get caught. I pull the headphones back over my ears and fix my eyes on the screen, forcing it back into focus.

He stands, pulling up his yellowed briefs and tucking himself in before he zips and buttons his pants. Somehow he managed not to further stain his ratty white v-neck. Looming over her, he presses a kiss to the top of her head. "Goodnight, be a good girl and say your prayers."

His broad shoulders block out the room's light as he strides toward the staircase.

"You know," he says, turning back, "I think next time, we might do something special. You're getting so big now. I think you might be ready for more."

Olivia stands frozen, shivering, naked.

I know, baby, I think at her. *I know it's hard, but you can do this. This is the last time, okay baby? I promise you, it's almost over.* I want that to be the truth so desperately.

Thinking the words feels like a lie. I'm not prepared. I don't even know what I want to do to him yet. How I plan to kill him. I don't want to put him down like I've done some of the others. I want him to suffer.

I will my strength into her. My courage, the coldness in my veins. I give it to her, knowing I will feel it later, but it's the only thing I can do.

She stands there for a long time, and I stay with her.

It's late when she forces herself to move.

She wipes her hands on the folded corner of her shirt, wraps it around the underwear and walks to the corner of her room. She pushes an old dollhouse out of the way, then opens the latch of the wall panel that seals off the attic.

Inside, on the floor, she adds the soiled bundle to the growing pile in the cupboard.

She closes the door, pulling fresh clothes from her dresser drawer. She tugs the clean T-shirt over her head, steps into clean purple underwear and curls into the corner of her bed, the overhead light still casting its sickly pallor over the room.

I sit up, watching over her as she shakes. I hear the tears and soft sighs. I listen when she goes silent and the solace of sleep sweeps over her, wiping her mind clear for the moment. Still, I stay with her 'til lavender light tints the skyline and her alarm for school sounds shrilly in my ears.

When she heads to the bus, I set my alerts and stretch out on my bed for a nap.

When I close my eyes, I know sleep is not enough to erase my memory of what I saw tonight.

THIRTEEN

Momma used to have brown eyes. Now they're cloudy and gray. She doesn't blink or answer me when I try to wake her up.

She never sleeps like this. Not on the floor where it's cold.

I smooth a bandage over the hole in her head, but blood comes out anyway. It's on the floor, the knees of my pants, my bare feet, and my hands. It's all around her still body.

The door to the coat closet gapes open. A trail of coats has fallen out, revealing my hiding place. Part of me wants to crawl back into the corner where I know I'll be warm and—there's a knock outside.

A lady opens the door before I can make it back to the corner of the closet. "Oh, sweetie, it's okay."

I recognize her from the bad days before. Momma's friend, Miss Percilla.

She doesn't leave the threshold of the front door. She doesn't touch my mother. She just reaches her hand out to me, grabs my wrist and pulls me toward her.

I try to get away, try to go back to Momma.

Some of the blood from my hands gets on her, but Miss Percilla holds me close to her chest. She's warm and smells good. She's wearing a simple dress with a soft sweater over it that she wraps around me as she shuts the door behind her.

It's cold outside.

I wish I had my coat, but it's too late to get it now. It's in the mess on the floor by the door where I was hiding.

She carries me back to her car. She holds me on her lap as she starts the car and drives away.

"I just need to find a pay phone," she says.

I don't ask, but I want to know what a pay phone is.

After a while, she stops at a grimy, old gas station.

There's a woman behind the counter with a salt and pepper mullet wearing blue coveralls that have grease stains all over them. She nods at Percilla, then turns and looks out the window.

I watch the woman over Percilla's shoulder as she carries me toward the bathrooms at the back of the store. We go into a room that has a big red stop sign on it.

She takes off her sweater and her simple dress and hangs them on a hook.

There are red stains on it where I touched it. I wonder if she's noticed them and worry she'll be angry if she does.

She is wearing a cream-colored turtleneck and jeans underneath the dress. She hangs her key next to the clothes and takes a different set off the hook. She helps me wash my hands and face in the old, rust-stained sink that looks really gross. She washes my feet. Then she takes off my dress and pulls a drab corduroy one over my tank top and panties. She buttons the dress down the front.

I hear voices in the store when we come out.

"The bathrooms are closed," the woman behind the counter says, sounding annoyed and bored.

Percilla guides me out of the nasty little closet, back toward the garage and a side door that has a different car parked next to it. She buckles me into a booster seat in the back. Then gets behind the wheel, backs out, and pulls onto the road.

I watch from the rear window as we leave the gas station behind.

There are dark cars with dark windows stopped around the gas station pumps. The car we came in is over there too.

Daddy is looking in the back window of that car.

He doesn't see me when I wave goodbye.

Percilla drives for a long time.

When we get to where she's been taking us, it's a single-story brick hotel with bars on the windows and gates that lock the inner courtyard to everyone who isn't supposed to be there.

She pulls the car into a garage, and we get out. She locks the doors with a key and carries me inside.

My alarm sounds.

I'm back in my van, lying in my queen bed with the blankets wrapped around my legs and sweat chilling my skin.

I haven't had that dream in a long time.

FOURTEEN

The next morning, I lock up the van, more out of habit than necessity. Around here, almost every vehicle has the keys tucked above the visor, in the center console, or tossed in the driver's seat.

There are three houses on this street.

Only two are occupied, and there's nothing else within five square miles, with acres of woods between.

Olivia heads to the bus stop at 7:00, she'll ride her bike to the shed at the end of the lane and take the bus from there.

A bus for her mother, Samantha, arrives at 8:30.

This is different. She must have an appointment today.

A health aide exits the vehicle and Eddy helps her out the back door until the aide takes over. Eddy gets in his car and heads to work.

I wait 'til the trail cam picks up his car on the way out before I start walking toward the house. There's a rusted-out fence in the tree line, but I've cut through it to make coming and going easier.

The grass is a little beat down from my passing, but I'll be out of here in a few days.

The plan is fairly simple.

Usually, I would observe for longer than the seven days it's been, but out here in the middle of nowhere, I have to make adjustments and work with what I have. Since they don't rely heavily on electronics, I'm not likely to get much more sitting outside the house. I hate the risk, but it is necessary.

Now that the mic is in place, I need to get into the house and get their schedule. Once I have it, I'll be looking for the next day when Samantha and Olivia are not at home, and Eddy will be there alone for the day.

Most people have a calendar on the fridge, a pad by the phone, or something in the office. I'm guessing that, since there are still some places out here where all you can get is dial-up, it won't be on the computer. That would be lucky. If it is digital, this may take a bit longer.

Once I know the day they'll be gone, I'll prep my setup.

I'm still trying to decide how I want to do things, but to be perfectly honest, I think he's going to have to suffer more than anyone else I've ever killed. I want him to beg for death, and when he's begging, I'll draw it out. Not because I enjoy suffering, but because he deserves it.

I adjust the gloves on my hands, the latex tacky in the heat. I've got a few extra pairs in my pockets. Always. And shoe covers. A must.

The door at the back of the house isn't locked, not that anything around here is. But it still feels odd to walk into the silent, empty house, the warmth from the side window in the kitchen fighting the window air conditioning unit in the living room.

There's a calendar on the fridge and a notebook next to the phone, but they don't have anything written on them. If Samantha has one, she must have taken it with her.

The house feels haphazard.

The kitchen is the only vaguely inviting living space. There's a basket of medication on the counter next to the fridge and a wheelchair by the couch. The only areas wide enough for it to turn around and navigate are the primary bedroom, the living room, and the hall connecting the two. There's a walker with a bench in the kitchen where Samantha can move between the two parts of the house and access the bathroom, but it's clear that this space was not designed with her mobility in mind.

The room she shares with Eddy is a decent size. There's a recliner in one corner, a large bed with head and footboard, and a long low dresser covered in clothes. Picture frames with the faces of friends and family glowering out from between the wadded up shirts and socks. One nightstand is cluttered and stacked with magazines, a worn Bible and a few beat-up books by some prophetess dressed in puritanical black and white.

Samantha's side of the room is tidy. A desk faces the lone window. The blinds are shuttered, blocking most of the light.

I peek through the shades. The casement faces the neighbor's house, though the building isn't visible from the angle she would be seated at. But there is a clear view of the old stable where they keep the family car and a few bikes.

I turn back to the room. While I'm inside, I should really look for weapons. Although the religion Eddy professes is a pacifist one, it's clear that he doesn't actually practice what he preaches.

FIFTEEN

I hear a car in the driveway at the same time I realize I muted notifications for the trail cam. But it is worse than I feared. Eddy is in the driver's seat, and Olivia is in the back, her bike shoved awkwardly into the trunk of the old station wagon.

The drive wraps around the porch, and cardboard boxes piled in the hall obstruct the front entrance, eliminating it as an exit option. It also blocks the side where I came in and cuts off my path to the neighboring house where my van is hidden.

I follow their progress past the front of the house and work my way toward the front hall.

A car door slams. His voice rumbles low enough that I can't hear what he is saying.

"Where's Mom?" Olivia's voice sounds shrill and concerned.

His answer is unintelligible.

"But why did you pick me up from school?"

Shit. Shit shit shit.

He had meant *today*.

There isn't a way for me to get out. Not without direct confrontation. And I haven't observed them long enough to say if he would try to protect her from me or use her as a shield. Would he send her to the other neighbor for help? They were far enough away that I hadn't spent much time on their routines, but in a hypothetical case, if I were in a physical altercation, there's no doubt that Olivia could make it to their house before I could catch her after handling Eddy.

I am completely unprepared. While I pride myself on my natural creativity, murder isn't a situation where winging it is beneficial. It makes the exit more difficult, and the risk increases exponentially.

Before the back door opens, I have one moment to make a snap decision. I start up the old creaking stairs before I can second-guess myself. Hopefully, the clatter of the kitchen door will mask the sounds, and the rooms between the back of the house and the stairwell will be enough to muffle my footsteps. The shoe covers don't do much for the noise, but they do cover footprints.

I'm halfway to the second floor when the screen door slams. I slow my pace to move in silence, gauging my success by the distance of their voices.

"I just don't understand why you pulled me out of school if Momma isn't home. I thought something was wrong. Don't you have work?"

I freeze as the living room door opens.

"Wait, Olivia, come back in here," he says.

The door doesn't close, but her voice is fainter.

When I reach the top of the stairs, I move to the room opposite Olivia's. If she comes upstairs, I don't want to startle her. The last thing I need is for her to give me away.

Glancing around, I remember this is Eddy's office.

It's dusty and a bit too warm. It's obvious he doesn't use this space more than he has to, but there's a large calendar mat on the desk. Fuck. It's too risky to try to write down anything right now. I step back into the corner, away from the doorframe, and into the shelter of the room. It's too late to use the information, anyway.

This is going to be much more complicated than I had expected. I can't think of a way to keep her from seeing me. Not if I intend to save her from this—and I do intend to do that. But then there's the issue of a witness. Would she tell anyone about me? Admit to there being someone else here if she does see me? I can't think about the other girls now. I can't think about saving anyone else. I'm already in the house. And if I'm caught?

No, he hasn't told anyone they're here. He didn't want anyone to know he was coming back home. That was the whole point. It was supposed to be the two of them all morning.

Her footsteps are light as she comes up the stairs, his plodding gait heavy behind her.

I'm out of time.

"I promised you we were going to do something, you and I. And after, if you behave, I've got popcorn, candy, and a movie for you."

"I don't want to do anything special. I just want to be normal."

"Olivia," his voice is warning, but I can't see his expression.

Shit. Should I have gone into her room instead? I hadn't expected him to chase her up here. There's no way for me to get him without trapping her in the room. I don't know if he has a gun. I didn't even have the chance to look for one in the house. When I left my van, I packed light—flashlight, notebook, and knife.

I look around the room for something, anything I can use to create a distraction as he herds her into her room, cutting off her escape.

"Take your clothes off," he says.

"No!" she screams at him. "I don't want to. I don't want this!"

"What did I say about being sweet?"

The clatter of footsteps—his heavy, hers light—and a short pursuit ends with the thud of a fall and a tearful plea for him to stop. It sounds like she's struck him.

"Little bitch," he says.

I snatch a dusty paperweight from the desk and slide it across the floor toward the stairs like a hockey puck.

It skates into the wall and falls, the echo reverberating up the hall as it strikes and drops from each riser on its descent.

The room across the hall goes quiet.

The floor groans as he stands.

Light footsteps skate toward me, and a body hits the other side of the wall where I'm hiding.

"Olivia!" he bellows.

His slower pace takes up the chase.

I untie the sleeves of my jacket from my waist and stand, wait 'til I hear him take two steps, I slip around the corner just as he turns to follow her down the flight. I loop it around his neck and jerk it down. I'm lucky. His foot catches the paperweight, and his feet go out from under him. I plant my feet on the wall panels on either side of the stairwell and pull as hard as I can.

The screen door bangs shut.

The house goes quiet.

Just me twisting the jacket tight in my grasp, and his shuffling movements as he tries to get away.

We stay like that for a while, 'til he goes quiet and still. There's a knot at the back of his head from the fall. A trickle of blood mats his hair, but he's still breathing.

She's gone. I hope she doesn't come back.

When I'm sure he's unconscious, I push him down the stairs, then follow on shaking legs. The door at the bottom of the landing leads to the primary bedroom. I open it and drag him in feet first.

It takes me a while to get him onto the bed and tie him to the frame, but once I've got him secured, I take a seat and catch my breath. Sweat beads on my brow, and I'm more tired than I like to be.

I check the house over.

The cordless landline is in the cradle, and the car keys are in a dish by the door. I peek out the back.

Olivia's backpack is still in the car. That's good. It means she's either hiding in the woods or in one of the outbuildings.

She hasn't seen me. Yet.

I lock the doors to keep her outside.

It's time for me to go to work.

SIXTEEN

I keep checking the time while I wait for him to wake up.

"Hey, sleepyhead," I say, when he opens his eyes.

"Who the fuck are you?"

I tsk. "Now, is that any way to speak to a lady? You've been very naughty, Edward. I came here to have a chat with you about it and see if we can't come to some kind of understanding."

"Where's Olivia?" He asks.

"Don't say her name."

He laughs.

"You left your pants upstairs," I gesture with the knife tip to the yellowed tighty-whities he's wearing. "Aren't your things down here?"

He grunts. "I don't have to explain myself to you."

I can tell he's angry, but he's trying not to show it. The indignity of being captured by a woman is too much for him to take, but his pride is still strong enough that he can't—or won't—admit it.

His nonchalance is pissing me off. His crime is serious, and for him to be more concerned with my gender means he hasn't yet realized how much danger he's in.

"What do you want?" he asks.

Finally, I can work with this. I don't respond to what he asks and instead say, "I'm glad you set things up so we could be alone."

"Bitch, I asked you a question."

"When I first learned what you were up to, how you were treating Olivia, there was one main thing I wanted to know. The answer to that is going to dictate how the next few hours go. Okay?" I phrase it as a question, but I don't need an answer from him. "Does Samantha know what you've done to her daughter?"

He grins. "No."

I smile. "Good." I breathe out a sigh of relief. "That's excellent. We can get started without her, and we'll be done before they get home. I really didn't want to make an orphan today. If she were in on it, she'd have to die, too."

His pupils widen. For the first time, his new reality seems to set in.

"Now, if you feel like you need to scream and cry, you just go on and do that. It won't bother me at all."

I check the clove hitches that secure him to the bed frame, making sure they're still snug, then I open my knife and angle the blade away from myself, tip toward him, sharp edge up to slice through the fabric of his shirt and yellowed underpants.

He tenses, expecting pain.

I'm not going to cut him. Not yet.

It's cooler in here than it is in the rest of the house. He shivers. I'm aware of his nakedness, but I ignore it for now, because no one really wants to see this. Not even him.

For a moment, I wonder if things in this room hold any sentimental value for Samantha, but then I realize I don't care. While she isn't guilty of the same things Eddy is, she is ignorant of her daughter's suffering, and I don't have any more compassion in my heart right now. I've given every ounce I had to Olivia.

I pace, gathering my thoughts. It's still early in the day, and since all this was a surprise, I'm feeling indecisive about my methods.

The worn Bible on his nightstand catches my eye. It's the classic King James Version. Scripture is something we have in common, though for different reasons. I enjoy the poetry of it.

He seems to use it as a weapon. Now, I will too.

I pick it up and leaf through it, noting the underlined portions. "I bet you wish I was one of those New Testament girlies," I say, flipping to Matthew. "I do think this is a good place to start, though. Then we can work backward. But I can't wait to go Old Testament on your ass."

"You blaspheme," he hisses.

"I do? Is that different from pedophilia?"

He does not meet my gaze.

I flip the pages 'til I find the chapter I'm looking for. "Matthew, chapter five, verse twenty-eight," I start. "But I say unto you, that whosoever looketh on a woman to lust after her hath committed adultery with her already in his heart."

He averts his eyes as I read verse twenty-nine. "And if thy right eye offend thee, pluck it out, and cast it from thee: for it is profitable for thee that one of thy members should perish, and not that thy whole body should be cast into hell."

His jaw flexes as he resists the urge to speak.

I read verse thirty. "And if thy right hand offend thee, cut it off, and cast it from thee: for it is profitable for thee that one of thy members should perish, and not that thy whole body should be cast into hell."

His brow furrows, and he glances at me when I close the book, but when I look up to meet his eye, he averts his gaze.

"Tell me, Eddy—Do you mind if I call you Eddy?" I let my focus bore into him, but he doesn't answer. "I'm going to call you Eddy. Now, I find it hard to believe that you are ashamed of what you've done. I open the Bible and read a few verses, and you can't even meet my eyes? But I know what you do. Is that what makes you afraid to look at me? Is it only when an adult knows your behavior, that you find your actions shameful? And it is shameful. What you've done."

I pace around the room, watching the changing lines of his face. "According to the passage I've read to you, I'm not sure where to start. Should I take out your eyes or cut off your hands? What was the first way you sinned? I don't mean to take your confession. I'm here to punish you. I'm here to cast your whole body into hell. Since I intend to do it properly, if you won't tell me where to start, I'll just have to go with my gut."

I pause for a while, waiting for him to say something, but he doesn't.

Disappointing.

"The last one wasn't a talker either—well, he couldn't talk, so maybe it was a little different. You know, I once thought you could just pop an eye out. I thought the globe could just hang there, only attached by the optical nerve, but that's not really how it works. You see, well, you can't yet—but imagine with me, there are a lot of muscles that hold your eye in place," I explain.

"I learned this by accident a bit ago, so you really have a lot to be thankful for because I won't make the same error. I ruptured his eye by mistake. I didn't know that most of the time, when there's a globe luxation—that's what they call it—a globe luxation and optic nerve avulsion, it's usually because there's an orbital fracture. Well, since I didn't know that, I didn't fracture his orbital—his orbit?" I frown. "Yes, his orbit."

Eddy shies away from me like I might actually hit him.

I laugh. It's funny that he imagines being hit is the worst thing that I will do to him.

"That's going to make it harder to pluck out the eye, but what we can do is detach the muscles first. That will let us pull it out without damaging the optic nerve. Of course, at some point, I will have to blind you, but we can talk about how we want to do that later. A lot of this is going to depend on how much time we have, but I'm optimistic. So, back to the eye. I don't have a scalpel. Usually, they do this with surgical scissors, forceps, and a scalpel, but since I only have this knife, I think I'll have to modify my approach."

He screams as I stick the knife in above his eyelid and the blade scrapes across the bone of his socket.

"You'll need to be still. I'm really not sure how close I am to your brain. I should have looked that up before…"

He draws a shaking breath and holds as still as he can, like he has hope he might get out of this alive.

I work the blade around his orbit, pressing a gloved hand up under his jaw to hold his head as still as possible. His moaning comes out strangled between pursed lips. When I'm done, his upper and lower lids rest uselessly over his eye. Blood pools in the corners and runs down his cheek and onto the pillow.

His breath come in gasps and shudders.

"Are you still with me, Eddy?"

He grunts, but that's confirmation enough for me.

"I'm a little worried, you know. This passing out on me, I'm not sure how much of this you'll get to experience, which is kinda the whole point." I sit beside him on the bed and pat his arm congenially.

He flinches and begins to cry.

I reach for his face, hesitate, then press my fingers into the socket and pluck out his eye.

He passes out.

SEVENTEEN

"Eddy!" I exclaim as he opens his left eye. "I'm so glad you're back! I was waiting on you. Since you were out, I decided to save some time and get you ready for the next step. Now, the Bible isn't super specific on how to do this one, but since I'm working with limited time and resources, I decided to be literal when the Bible says, 'cut off your hand and cast it away.' So that's what I'm going to do, but I did take the liberty of switching from the clove hitch to a Prussia knot. I think it will be a bit better cause it might double as a tourniquet, and we don't want you bleeding out… yet."

"I'm begging you," he whispers, "I swear, I'll never do it again."

I smile. "No, Eddy. I know you won't." I lean toward his face, making sure he can see with his good eye how serious I am. "That's because I'm here to stop you."

I always carry a sturdy knife, which is a good thing because cutting off a hand is a tough job.

Luckily, I can borrow the hatchet from the firewood when it comes time to break the bones. I start cutting above the wrist joint. It's easier to disarticulate at the joint than to sever the limb and break the bone. And I'm pretty sure this will be more painful.

He screams at the first cut of the blade, but I push through 'til he passes out again.

There's a monotonous lull when he's unconscious and I'm sawing through fascia, fat, muscle, and tendon, but the bleeding isn't as bad as I had expected.

I'm not terribly good with the hatchet, and Eddy wakes up when I'm still hacking at his arm. That's when the screaming really gets serious. He glares at my handiwork and starts thrashing, which causes even more damage.

"Now, Eddy, I'm not very good at amputations when I don't have my kit. And I'm still an amateur under those circumstances, so it would be best if you kept still."

"Oh my God, please!" he screams.

I pause my cutting and sigh. "Are you finished?"

"Please stop, for the love of God, please!"

I bend back to my work and after a few more well-placed hits, I'm able to snap the hand free. It isn't clean, but I'm more than ready to move on by the time it comes off.

I'm glad I wore my shoe covers and gloves. An early lesson in breaking and entering is "always be prepared." Plus, it keeps the evidence to a minimum, no fingerprints, no shoe prints, no tracking bits from one crime scene to the next.

I'm sweating, not pouring, but the tacky kind that covers my body and makes me feel like I'm starting to stink, and the rust smell on my clothes makes me miss my painter's suit. I'll need a good shower after this. I'm more worried about the blood than anything. Even if they do find some of my DNA, they don't have anything to run it against. I just don't want to get any stains in the van.

I'm a little worried that I'm already feeling fatigued after removing only the eye and the hand. I glance at the clock. Almost *1:30*. I'm not going to be able to do everything I want to.

By the time I start on his foot, I'm getting bored. He is passing out and coming to every few minutes, and I have a feeling he needs fluids if he is going to make it much longer.

Disappointing.

It occurs to me that being able to administer fluids intravenously might be a good skill to have in my line of work. For multiple reasons.

"I couldn't find anything specific for your feet. If I had more time, we would have had a full itinerary, and I'd have gotten some fluids for you. But you just couldn't wait, could you?"

His eye rolls around the socket bleary and dazed. Sweat beads on his temple, and he moans a reply.

"God, I feel like I keep fucking this up," I grasp his left wrist with my index and middle finger checking his pulse. It's high and fast. That and the clammy sweat show he's in shock.

I'm running out of time.

I check the clock. It's just after *2:00*. I decide to skip ahead.

I put the knife down and head for the kitchen to get some extra tools. They aren't what I'd normally reach for, but I have to work with what I've got.

A knife sharpener, hatched metal forming a rough surface. I grab a wooden spoon, and an ice pick from the drawer by the fridge, an assortment of utensils that don't seem to be used.

He's still conscious and shaking when I come back to the room. His eye goes wide when he sees the items in my hands.

"Well, Eddy," I say with a smile, "I've got some things for you, but I couldn't find verses for what I'm going to do next. Then again, I can't find verses for some of what you did, either."

I pause and take a deep breath. "Now, we're going to get a bit more serious."

EIGHTEEN

The fear in his eye seems to expand, and the stink of his sweat makes it clear that he is the hunted.

The bitter smell of urine fouls the air.

I reach into my back pocket and pull out another pair of gloves, mentally preparing for what I'm about to have to do.

I pull the bedclothes off, leaving only the fitted sheet beneath him. I rip the pillows from under his head. When I retie his right leg, cinching it further toward the edge of the bed, then move to the left leg. There's a bit of slack for his arms, but not enough to concern me. I focus intently on my goals. If this part were easy, it would make me just like him.

If I got any pleasure or joy from this kind of torture, I would have to be next on my own list, but I'm not that kind of person. I remind myself that I'm still good. But someone has to make the abusers pay, and there's no one to do that but me. My penance is the suffering I see on all sides. That is what makes my heart pure. I take the metal sharpener in hand and turn to him.

He's a little aroused, half limp, and he tries not to meet my gaze, but he likes being inappropriate. For as much shame he has brought into this house, there is always more that the perverse mind craves.

But I'll make sure he gets no joy from this.

Anger flashed in me at the sight of him, even in this weakened state, still finding some kind of pleasure. A reminder that no matter what I do, he must die.

Men like him must always die.

I grasp his penis and testicles in one gloved hand, twisting and lifting as he cries out in shocked pain.

"No, no, please, not that, just kill me!"

He doesn't realize that it's not the knife I hold in my hand.

I ram the sharpener into his anus, feeling the tug of skin as my aim is not perfect, but near enough the mark that I'm able to force it in part of the way. I release his genitals and palm my hand over the handle of the sharpening rod, then hit it with my fist 'til it shifts further inside him. I feel more tearing as he shrieks and gasps in pain.

I feel cold, physically, listening to his screams, the high-pitched wheeze that sounds as he tries to breathe in.

For the first time in our brief acquaintance, he thrashes against his bindings. It pulls me back into my body. At the sight of his anger, I see clearly that, given the right leverage, he would have become physically violent with them. I don't even want to think their names. Not with the vile things that have happened here in this house.

I grab my knife and grasp his penis in a gloved hand, lifting it up with my left hand and draw the blade across the base, cutting it away from his body.

His scream is bloodcurdling.

I'm glad for the rubber gloves. They make it easier to keep a good grip when he begins to bleed. I adjust my grip and follow the curve of his pubic bone, cutting down around his scrotum so his testicles are peeled like grapes. I leave the ducts attached.

When he has stopped screaming, and I'm sure he's conscious, I grasp the flesh of his testicles, leaving the skin, and jerk down firmly 'til they come away in my hand and the tubes pop free. It's kind of like they do with hogs, but with animals, they cut the cords and leave the penis. Since I'm dealing with a pig, I don't bother.

"Now, Eddy, I want you to look in the mirror, see what I've done. I want this to be the last way you see and remember yourself." I grab the mirror from the vanity and turn it toward him so he can see himself, his missing eye, hand, and genitals.

I take one of his testicles and place it in his empty socket.

He shrieks, his mouth contorting as he sobs.

I hold his head still and shove his severed penis into his mouth, forcing him to watch in the mirror.

He gags.

I take the knife in hand and start on extracting his other eye. I'm working quickly now.

His sniveling cries are a vague distraction. He has not fainted in a while. I'm surprised, but pleased.

I realize that there is a bit of the show he will have to miss, but that cannot be helped.

I open his Bible, my bloody hands leaving smears on the delicate pages as I search for my place.

"Judges, chapter four, verse twenty-one," I read to him. "Then Jael Heber's wife took a nail of the tent, and took an hammer in her hand, and went softly unto him, and smote the nail into his temples, and fastened it into the ground: for he was fast asleep and weary. So he died."

He makes a gagging sound around the organ in his mouth.

I look up from the Bible. "I can see where I could have followed these instructions a bit more clearly. Ah, that may have been a poor choice of words, but we got there in the end. Since you won't be able to see the final project, I figured, I can still tell you about it. And while I went a bit further than the biblical foreskin, I think it was along the same lines as the first few verses we read, so overall this was a success. Now, I am going to leave enough evidence here that it will be pretty clear what you have been doing to them. Other than that, what do you say we wrap this up?" I laugh. "Not that you have anything to wrap up anymore!"

He moans.

"I didn't realize your sense of humor was in your pants. Someone should research that!" I have a delirious sense of relief washing over me, leaving me feeling a bit slaphappy, but the worst is over.

I keep reminding myself of that.

I kneel on the bed beside him, leaning forward until I can get the right leverage. He hardly fights me when I turn his head so I can access his temple. I place the ice pick against his head, cup the wooden handle, then bring my fist down hard on my hand. I'm surprised at how quick it is.

His body seizes and rattles a bit, but then he goes still.

I step back off the bed. Looking at the room, the blood-stained Bible still beside him on the bed, the heap of soiled linens, and blood-smeared mirror, I know there is no cleaning this up.

I turn his head so his face is looking toward the ceiling, then place one testicle in each socket and replace his penis in his mouth.

I change my gloves, open the door, and run upstairs to her room.

I open the wall panel and carefully pull out an armload of Olivia's pajamas and underwear. It's too much to take all of it, but I leave the hiding spot open so they can see what was there. I leave a trail of them through the house. From the wall panel behind the dollhouse, out into the upstairs hall, down the stairs, and into the room where he is.

I leave the rest on the bed beside him.

There's a lot of them.

Too many.

When I'm done, I step back and take it in one more time.

My knife. I need to find my—it's there on the nightstand. I put it in my pocket, then peel off the outer layer of gloves. It's going to be interesting trying to get myself cleaned up before I get in the van, but first, I need to do something about the girl.

NINETEEN

I need to move quickly. I'm covered in blood. I don't have time to see how badly, but at least black hides the stains pretty well.

I take off another layer of gloves and pull a trash bag from under the kitchen sink. I put the gloves in it, then bend over and remove the shoe covers, too.

I glance around the house one more time, then open the door and walk out into the sunshine. It's a hot afternoon. The buzz of bees fills the air, and flies zip by. I imagine I smell like a buffet to them.

Olivia isn't immediately visible when I reach the back door.

I head for the tree line with the broken fence, carrying the bag. I'm not sure if she saw me before, but if she didn't, there is a good chance she is watching me now. Maybe not, though. She stood still dissociating for a long time last night…

If they ask her what happened, maybe she won't say anything about me. I can't count on it.

I am careful not to brush against anything as I make my way through the trees and back to the van, glad I parked it in such a good location. Once I am hidden behind the van and the wrecked cars, I get out another heavy-duty trash bag, and step into it to strip off most of my clothes. As much as I hate to get rid of anything, these will have to be burned as soon as possible.

I haven't been here long enough to know where she would go. I didn't even take the time to scout the outbuildings. Stupid mistake. I thought I'd have more time.

It doesn't matter now. Hindsight being what it is—useless—'til I get out of this situation.

So it would be a place she can get to quickly without being followed. A small space, maybe, or a difficult path for him to follow.

Not the building closest to the house.

Or the horse barn up at the front of the property, on the other side of the drive. It would have to be the one further back toward the tree line, closer to me and the junkyard where I am.

I put on gloves and a clean painter's suit over my underwear, combine all the trash bags, then pull a dark sweatshirt over top so the white doesn't look so conspicuous.

Sliding into the driver's seat of my van, I aim my binoculars at the side building looking for any movement and wait. Minutes go by, and still there's nothing. I take out my infrared scanner and aim it at the building. Nothing. It doesn't look like she was ever in there.

I scan the tree line again, looking for any other potential hiding places, but the other buildings all have easy access and seem too unlikely. There is one place though, not a building really, a cross between a hunting blind and a treehouse. I aim the binoculars at the tree across the driveway in front of the large front porch.

Olivia has her knees drawn up on the narrow platform. The ladder of two-by-fours nailed into the tree looks like it's nearly rotted out, but her back is against the trunk and there's a slanted roof over her head. The sides are partly opened, but leave a narrow gap where the trunk of the tree rounds away from the wooden panels that would shelter her from a light rain if there were any. But that's a good bet with the sky as overcast and gray as it has been.

After a while, she unfolds her legs and lets one hang over the edge of the platform as she shifts. More time goes by, and she switches to the other leg, stretching that as well.

I change position in my seat, realizing I'm getting stiff too, and I've been watching her for less than half an hour.

Finally, the short white bus with red and blue lettering turns in at the end of the road. I wait as it drives past the doublewide and virtual junkyard where I'm parked and drives up to the old white farmhouse I'm watching. They pull around to the side of the house where the kitchen door faces the backyard. I have a good clear view of it when one of the health aides steps out in his light blue scrubs and knocks on the kitchen door.

I pan over to where Olivia is sitting. She's moved a little, twisting in her seat so she can look back toward the house, though from her angle, I can't imagine she sees very much.

The aide knocks on the door again.

Of course, there is no response. I hold my breath when the driver steps out of the bus and joins the aide in blue scrubs.

The driver opens the storm door and tries knocking again, then he tries the knob.

It isn't locked.

Blue Scrubs props the door open, and they go back to the bus together and start to help a woman, who must be Samantha, out.

Her chair doesn't fit in the house if it's not folded.

This morning, Eddy helped bundle her off through the door, swapping an indoor chair for the outdoor one, then folding the second chair away for storage once she was in the care of the aides.

Even from this distance, I can see irritation in their movements.

They try to force it.

What the fuck am I going to do if they break her chair? I can almost guarantee she won't have the money to replace it without Eddy.

She holds up a hand to stop them. Surprisingly, they listen. Then, Blue Scrubs disappears into the house.

I hold my breath.

Moments later, the man bursts out the door and hunches over the flower bed.

It wasn't something I calculated for, though it seems obvious now. I hadn't gotten as far as how I planned to kill him, let alone who was going to find the body. While I never want to traumatize innocent people, sometimes it is unavoidable.

I shift my focus back to Olivia. She still hasn't moved, and I'm starting to feel unsettled.

Samantha is waving her hands around. Although I can't hear what she is saying, her distress is evident.

The driver has his phone out and is trying to make a call, but there's no cell reception. Finally, he goes into the house. Another passenger with a cane comes to the door of the bus, but doesn't get out. Blue Scrubs waves a hand at him, gesturing in the universal sign to stay put.

After a while, the driver comes back holding a portable house phone to his cheek. He starts to gesticulate too, then offers the phone to Samantha. She takes it. Then the driver and Blue Scrubs start walking around the house, hands cupped to their mouths, shouting.

I roll my window down a little, trying to hear what they are saying, though I think I already know what it is. They're looking for Olivia.

When she climbs down from her perch, crosses the creek and the driveway, and gets back to the house, I put the van in reverse and navigate out of my hiding spot. By the time I reach the end of the road, my heart rate has picked up. I'm antsy from waiting, not being able to leave when I know I should be running.

I pull over and sprint to the tree line to retrieve my trail cam, then get back in the van. As I turn onto the main road, lights and sirens crest the hill in front of me. I pull to the shoulder and wait as two cars fly past, then a fire truck, then an ambulance.

The last one makes me chuckle. They're not going to need that. They should have sent a coroner instead.

It takes me twenty-five minutes to make it to I40. It will take about another hour and a half, driving the speed limit, to get to Nashville. From there, I'll hang a left and head up to Kentucky.

I haven't decided where I want to go after that, but I'll choose the closest state that isn't Arkansas, Alabama, or Tennessee.

I won't be coming back.

ABBY

TWENTY

Most of the time, I don't let my curiosity get the best of me. But today, I turn the radio on and listen for any news about what I've been up to.

But there's nothing yet on a gruesome killing in middle Tennessee.

I relax in my seat a little and flip the station to NPR. The news segment jingle plays, and it's relaxing. Familiar.

Traffic picks up as I get closer to the city, and I settle into the monotony of a long drive. I get off the interstate for gas at one of the big trucking stops even though the tank is still half full. And since I'm already there, I grab a burner phone from the bin under my bed. I put on a ball cap before I go inside and keep my head down, but I need a bag of candy, anything soft, chewy, and sour. While no one else is in the bathroom, I take the opportunity to shove the gloves in my pocket and properly wash my hands.

I pay cash at the counter, start the pump, then climb into the driver's seat to avoid the oppressive noise of the ads that play as soon as they have a semi-captive audience.

No thanks.

I squeeze hand sanitizer into my palm, then rub my hands together before starting on some of the candy. I want Percilla to tell me everything is going to be okay. That we're okay. I've been torn between driving to Virginia to see if there's anyone in that tiny town who knows me and listening to what Percilla said about being found.

The pump clicks off, and I get out to hang up the nozzle.

A cop car pulls in at the far end of the lot, and I pull my cap further down over my face even though I know I'm too far away for them to see me.

Time to get back on the road.

There's not a lot in this part of Kentucky, but I make a stop in Corbin. There's a shelter there that's part of Percilla's network where I can drop by. I know they won't bother me and I'm in desperate need of a shower.

While the shelter workers don't know what I do, they know I can skip the interviews and intake process on Percilla's word. And, sometimes, half of keeping people safe is not asking too many questions. Knowing too much about the people you're helping or who's helping you can be dangerous.

Percilla is big on this.

She keeps her records and makes the appropriate reports, but she knows people who've lost people at places like this. Some guy gets angry, follows his girl to a shelter, then kills the wrong person because if he can't have her, no one can. That type of shit. That's why we don't share too much.

I know Percilla has come close.

She has the scars to prove it, even if she doesn't talk about it much.

I guess I was the one time she broke her rules.

I think that turned out okay.

I don't have a particular timeframe. I call once I feel like I'm safe and as confident as I can be that I won't bring any trouble home with me.

Sure, the shelter line is a general phone number, but that doesn't mean we need anyone snooping around there either.

We keep our work as separate as we can.

I call Percilla.

Once she knows it's me, she asks. "How are you?"

"You were right. It was bad. Anything on the news about it?"

"Nothing," she says. "It will take some time. If it's not a pretty white girl out here, they don't care much about it, and he was an ugly son-of-a-bitch on a good day. They'll be more interested if anyone else was involved with him. Plus, they have to question the wife."

"Part of me hopes I didn't make it too bad for her, but part of me feels like she should have known something was wrong."

"Even if she was suspicious, he set it up so she couldn't check on him and see what he was doing," she says. "Abusers are really good at picking victims. A mother who needs help and can't seem to catch a break, a little girl who loves her mother and wants to protect her—wants her to have the help she needs. Abusers can spot things like that in people. They know what they're doing. They do it on purpose."

I try not to cry, but hearing her talk like that works out something in my heart that has been eating at me. The guilt, blame, and shame that keep people stuck in situations like this get to me, too. "I just feel like I should have been there sooner, like I should have done more."

"And what about Corrin?" she asks. "The only way you get to Olivia sooner is if you don't help Corrin first, right? It's just you and me. We're working as fast as we can, but we can't save everyone from everything. Yes, Olivia is going to be traumatized, she's going to need therapy, but now that people know what's happened, she's safe. She will have an opportunity to get those services."

I sniff hard, trying to hold back the sobs that are building in my chest. This wasn't why I called. For therapy and a pep talk.

We're quiet, the sound of my sniffing punctuating the silence.

"Abby, I'm really starting to worry about you. I think maybe we should slow down a bit. You're dealing with a lot. This kind of stuff causes PTSD. It would be good for you to take it easier. You've been doing so much of this on your own. I'm doing my best to have your back from here, but there's a lot of this, a lot more support you need, just as a person."

"We can't bring anyone else in on this," I reply. "You know that." It would be too dangerous.

"I'm not saying we bring someone else in. I'm just saying, since we can't do that, the only other thing we can do is give you more time in between jobs."

I huff out a snotty laugh and wipe my nose with my sleeve. "I'll take more time off if you tell me more about my father."

"That's the last thing you need right now." She doesn't even sound angry when she says it.

That's how I know she's really worried about me. Enough that I should be worried about me, too.

TWENTY-ONE

While I have more mandatory free time, I use my personal silver laptop to search for Tara Jackson again. This is how I see my mother, visiting her image because I can't go to her grave. She looks different from what I remember. Young and happy. Her dark curly hair is like mine. She has warm brown eyes, and I realize I've never been able to picture her this way since my father killed her. Even in my good memories of her, there's always a shadow in her gaze that's missing from this photo.

I can see why I was drawn to Corrin so much, too. She and my mother have the same bronzed skin and warm eyes. Only my mother chose the bad boy in a small country town. I wonder what drew my parents to each other.

I stare at the screen for a long time, trying to imagine all of us being happy together as a family.

After a while, I look up my name, too.

Mara Jackson.

It feels strange, just typing in my name.

There isn't as much about me. No graduation photos or cheer squad in the newspaper. There's a small gray picture that has been photocopied so many times that it doesn't look like me. Probably my school picture from kindergarten.

I don't remember it at all. It could be me. Then again, maybe not.

The scanned image is from a flyer for a missing girl. Mara Jackson. It comes from Georgia. When I try to find one for Virginia, I don't see any relevant results.

I scroll through a list of missing people from Virginia. Tara Jackson isn't on that list. They know what happened to her, but there are a lot of other women on there. Children, too. People whose faces don't make the news. I close my laptop and rub my eyes. Even though I know I need a break (Percilla is right about that), I can't stop thinking about this, my past.

Something about it is off. There are records I see in Georgia that should exist in Virginia, but there's nothing there.

According to the state of Virginia, everything might as well be fine. But regardless of what they say, I know Mara Jackson wasn't kidnapped on a family vacation. That isn't how I would describe Percilla rescuing me. Legal or not.

Everything about this stinks.

I try again, this time looking for the newspaper article. The full version of the trimmed one Percilla was hiding.

The article is in the special edition with an obituary for Judge Vernon Jackson. The paper is from Orange, Virginia. The full article doesn't make it any clearer which Jackson is Roland, my father. And Percilla isn't talking.

In a small town, you'd think there would be more talk about a situation like this.

Stranger still, there aren't any family photos of the Jacksons online, though it's abundantly clear that this family has no relation to the Stonewall or the Hermitage Jacksons.

I understand their legal and public records being gone. A lot of small towns have lost their archives to rodents, floods, and fires. The weird thing is how much effort has gone into removing any personal data for these Jacksons—information that is usually readily available on the internet.

For a family cosplaying as pillars of the community, It's odd that there are no social media accounts or newspaper mentions. Thinking about the kind of people who have the influence to disappear that much data makes the hair on my arms stand on end.

I stretch out on the bed, pressing my feet against the wall of the van, and look up at the ceiling, trying to clear my head.

Maybe it's not that strange. After all, I don't have any social media either. There haven't been any school photos, newspaper articles, or legal documents for Mara Jackson since I started being me. And as Abby, I don't have any of those things either, for obvious reasons.

Not that everyone who doesn't have social media is a criminal, but aside from being very private, I can only think of one reason a whole family would make such an effort to go completely dark online.

I sit up, getting a head rush from moving so fast.

The next job comes as a surprise. For once, I'm not excited to get back to work.

ANONYMOUS

Dear mercy,

I'm not sure if you help people like me, but if you do, I need your help. I don't feel like I can ask anybody I know. They think I'm being dramatic or maybe I should 'suck it up' but it's not that simple.

If it was just hitting, I think that I would be okay with it, but there's a lot more to it than that. I could deal with a bit of pain. I could even deal with the verbal stuff, but for my child—I think you know, I would do anything. But if I act myself, I'm afraid I'll make things worse.

From one parent to another.

TWENTY-TWO

Her name is Gloria. A perfect bottle blonde from what I can tell so far. They are the country club type with a his-and-hers garage and freshly washed and detailed red luxury crossovers. One week in and he seems to be perfect.

The first thing that strikes me is the age difference, but I am already wary of them. Usually, the letters aren't like this, and after the run I've been having, I'm planning to take my time and be extra careful.

Just getting into this neighborhood has been a pain. It seems like everyone actually talks to each other like it's fucking Mayberry. And Matt never leaves the house without Gloria. Actually, I haven't seen Matt leave the house at all.

Gloria is a woman about town, though. She has brunch dates every weekend, house guests, shopping sprees, and Matt to unload her purchases when she gets home.

They don't look like they are in love. There isn't even a visible pretense of it. He seems more like the help, who I assume sleeps in the same bed as her. Which is odd. I am also surprised that she is the one who is older.

From everything I can find, it says she is fifty-three.

He is twenty-five.

Percilla hasn't included anything about either of their work.

Gloria doesn't seem to have any kind of job, and he seems to spend all his time on household tasks. They are both busy, but I can't figure out where the money came from.

She has at least one other car, but I haven't been able to get a good look in the garage. I'm not even sure if he can drive.

Gloria is five feet two inches tall if she is wearing socks, but she never does. She is always in heels. It is all very *Gone With the Wind*, in a new money kind of extravagance that shouts, "Look at me, I'm so wealthy."

It's a little uncomfortable to think I may be on course to make more money from donations than some of the people I've been dealing with. What am I supposed to do with that?

Skimming the packet Percilla sent, I can't help noticing this one is a little thin. Something is up with this couple, but I can't figure it out. The money, the house, the cars, it's all just a little off in a way that doesn't give him away, like he's not overt with what he's doing.

If it were financial abuse, I wouldn't expect the cars to be in her name. Or for her to be driving, for that matter, but she seems perfectly independent.

I've not seen a mark on either of them.

I comb through the financials again. They always say, "follow the money." And I do, especially since there isn't anything else to pursue.

That's when I find the holding company.

It has several other properties under it. Oddly, the house they're currently staying at is the only one that is directly in her name. Each of the other properties are under a different LLC and nested in a larger holding that, in a roundabout way, traces back to a holding group she has shares in. His name isn't on anything.

So what does he do that he doesn't want his name on? It looks like he's set her up perfectly to be the fall guy for something big.

That's not to say a woman of her age can't pull a beautiful young man, but why would she want to?

It's obvious the money is hers.

I'm a bit frightened for her. Lots of men kill for money.

She should be wary and lock down all her assets so he can't get any of her things.

I look back at the letter to Mother Mercy.

It doesn't make sense. The request for help doesn't mirror what I'm seeing at all, and I have to remind myself, this is why I look at things. This is why I go in and shadow and make damn sure the abuser is actually an abuser and someone isn't just wielding me like a weapon to do more harm to someone who is already suffering.

This may be all I get out of the packet. There are some truths that can't be captured in a dossier like this.

I'm going to have to look for myself.

There's something else, too. I check again now that I'm looking at their details and the letter, I can't figure out who the parent is. I can't find any record of the Rubins having a child.

If they *did*, I might already be too late.

TWENTY-THREE

It is tricky to get a view inside the house. I am still working on a way in when it happens, so I didn't actually see. I didn't even have audio, which is maybe the worst part, so I didn't realize anything had happened until the ambulance arrived.

When they wheel him out on the stretcher, I can't be sure of what is wrong. The white sheet is pulled up over his legs, and he is buckled to the cot with two large paramedics guiding the gurney.

Gloria is a dutiful wife. She exits through the garage–still perfectly put together–speaks to the paramedics for a moment, then gets into her car and follows the ambulance away.

I use the opportunity when they are gone to work on getting into the house.

It's big for two people, but not as big as the Alabama monstrosity. This one has a black facade with large floor to ceiling windows that are treated with a reflective coating that makes it impossible to see in. It is more like a compound, with an iron fence and rich wood paneling that matches the siding on the house. The whole thing has an overtly modern feel that is aggressive and not at all welcoming. It is odd for a street where the rest of the houses feature pools and open concepts with outdoor kitchens and patio fire pits. Everyone else regularly has neighbors over, but this house is more or less closed for the season.

The tops of the fences are capped with small spear points, so going over the fence isn't going to work. It's tall enough that it's too risky for me. I've seen some things.

There are cameras, too. They cover most of the property, certainly any way a person might try to get in or out. The gate seems to be controlled by the same system that runs the cameras, and all of it is managed by a private security firm that I have absolutely no desire to tangle with. Not only would it make things very dangerous for me, there's no way I would be able to finish the job while also looking over my shoulder.

I rub my eyes with the heels of my palms, trying to refocus. I need to find a new approach.

Four hours later, they're back. No one gets through the E.R. that fast, but they must have a special connection because they are back from the hospital in less time than most people have to wait. His right foot is in a boot. She has on dark glasses that cover half her face.

The gate opens as they pull up to it. She turns into the gap and circles the driveway. The iron bars swing closed as she backs into the garage. The door slides down, and they disappear into the house.

I'm no wiser than I was this morning when I started.

As the sun begins to set, the various neighbors come out, gathering around their fire pits and settling into hot tubs.

Which reminds me that getting in isn't the only way to get information. Usually, I need to go in so I can see the abuse. My standard is the same as in any criminal court. *Beyond a reasonable doubt.* I can swear to it on a stack of Bibles, and while they're most likely to offend when they think that no one is watching, there has to be somewhere else they will willingly show their colors.

People smoke out bees for a reason.

I open the file on the laptop again and look over the information Percilla sent me. This isn't their only house. One of the others isn't far from here. It's in Virginia, too, near a place I've been wanting to visit very much. Now I just need to figure out how to get them to go there.

TWENTY-FOUR

I head to a secondhand store in search of fabric samples. Anything will do. I find a mix of bags that have cut squares of fabric and get several pieces so I can make a large sample of swatches. It doesn't have to look good. I'm aiming for out-of-fashion interior design.

I go the extra mile and add a page of sales copy, thanking the customer for their request and encouraging them to reach out with any questions. Of course, the number I include is out of service. On the surface, the whole thing looks semi-professional.

After I finish the first step, I start hunting for what I'm really after.

It takes several locations before I find what I need, but after the third seedy pay-by-the-hour motel, I find the sweet musky odor I'm looking for. They probably won't notice or care that I cut a square of the fabric cover from between the mattress and the box spring.

I'm careful to pack everything up before I take off the suit I'm wearing. The last thing I want is to get my van infested. That would be a worst-case scenario. I layer the fabric with the square of the mattress cover in the middle, then pack the whole thing into a bag and tape it into a box, securely sealed. The idea makes me itch, but it's not stupid if it works.

Even if it doesn't start what I'm hoping it will, the thought of it should be as noxious to them as it is to me.

Bedbugs are the worst, and I think a convincing risk of exposure will do the trick.

Since this kind of establishment doesn't have working cameras, I don't worry about being outside while I finish up my arts and crafts project. People here are just as interested in not being seen as I am. Nobody looks twice when I come out of the room and remove the painter's suit I'm wearing. I put this one right into a trash bag, then into the dumpster near the front of the building.

I'm not taking any chances.

Now that I have the package, getting the sample into the house might be trickier.

With the iron fence being the main barrier to a hand-delivered package, I mull over a few different options. Throwing it would probably get a bit too much attention. Even if they don't notice, there are a lot of cameras around here. There's also no way I'm going to ring the intercom. Paying off a neighborhood kid around here is too risky. A drone package delivery could be a lot of fun, but I don't *have* a drone, and now doesn't seem like the best time for the investment. I'd still have to learn how to fly it.

In this case, simple is probably best, so I settle for a local courier service. Wearing a wig and ball-cap when I take it in is the simplest way to not draw too much attention. I take the package into their office and use a burner email to send them a custom label for a fake company. The teen behind the counter couldn't care less, and his disinterest gives me an unexpected sense of comfort about the whole situation.

Now, I just have to give it a few days for things to ripen. After that, I can kick off the second part of my plan.

The most effective lies are the ones that are built on truth. For example, bedbugs are highly contagious. And if an outbreak is reported in an area, it is important they are treated.

Who starts the report is a bit more… fuzzy. But I find it most effective to leave the pest control company to report it to those who may be impacted. They have a better cause to promote fumigation than I do.

And, it turns out, Bug Out Bait and Bombs is *very* invested in getting their foot in these doors.

The salesman I speak to promises discretion. And gushing about my embarrassment over the second-hand antique furniture is effective, if a little over the top.

The next morning, he shows up in a suit and tie with a clipboard and a respectable sedan that makes no reference to keeping bedbugs at bay.

He works his way down the street, door to door, with what I'm hoping is a very convincing pitch.

He isn't aware of the legwork I've already done on his behalf.

A few hours later, Matt backs the car out of the garage.

So, he can drive.

He goes back inside and comes out again, carrying a black garbage bag to the bin behind a privacy fence, then he gets into the driver's seat and waits.

Twenty minutes later, Gloria walks down the front steps, gets into the car, and they're officially on their way.

TWENTY-FIVE

The country house is in rural Virginia, a several hours' drive from the coast. This place isn't listed under property records, but it is fairly easy to tail them from one house to the other.

And it is much better for surveillance.

It is, like all the other ranches in this part of the country, not far from Montpelier. Acres of green pasture behind wooden fences, red barns with references to Rock City, and tobacco fields with rust-colored soil in between. There are a few modern ranch houses, but the larger estates are the sprawling plantation-style houses.

Renovated slave cabins, which have been carved off the plantations—on stolen indigenous lands—are common, too. Often with antique farm equipment, long out-of-use silos, and dilapidated barns. The houses are mostly rentals, but the land still belongs to the old families, in one form or another.

The drive they pull into is at least a half-mile long. I hang back, keeping to the road and looking for a place to park that isn't too far away. It would be easy to be spotted here. Even though it is in the country, the roads are still busy.

Paper maps are a good cover for a tourist lost with spotty cell reception. Where even *is* James Madison's home and what time does the museum open? I keep the questions on the tip of my tongue as cover.

I find a place to park nearby at a house that's been locked up for the summer. I'm feeling especially grateful for people who post travel pictures while they're on vacation.

The end of this drive has a turnaround that is shaded with willow trees and right behind a curved stone wall that has the property name on it. Marvelous Meadows. It's a bit try-hard, but I can see what they were going for. There are a few remaining antebellum mansions around here that span thousands of acres, but if you can't find one for sale, the next best option is to build a pale imitation. What's better than a house that screams "ethical slavery, but make it aesthetic"?

This is the perfect place to park.

The driveway Gloria and Matt drove down is obliquely opposite and, as long as there isn't a secret, hidden exit somewhere else, I'll be able to see them coming and going.

I set up a camera facing the end of the drive and slap a magnet on the side of the van for Sure Home Security.

Aside from the occasional passing car, everything has gone quiet since rush hour has ended.

As much as I hate hiking, it seems that's going to be the best way to get a view of the property and find out what the big house is like. At least the ticks aren't too bad, and the hills are rolling instead of steep climbs. There is the occasional hedge and Civil War-era stone wall, but it's fairly easy to move through the underbrush here. Invasive privets have edged out the blackberry and raspberry bushes, making it a less thorny endeavor.

After packing some cameras, I hang my binoculars around my neck, pull on my backpack, and don a hat for a nonexistent bird watching club. Next, I lock the van, and start into the woods.

TWENTY-SIX

The large barn on the property is the farthest from the house and the easiest to get into. Since I found such a good place to park, I can afford to spend a few hours watching the building. Once I see their new schedule, I'll be able to make a more solid plan.

I figure if I get cameras up in the outbuildings first, I can pick my way in closer with a better understanding of how many people operate this place, where they are and when they work. It seems that the crew is thin to begin with, and the few people who do work here are further away from the house.

But I've learned my lesson since Olivia's case.

I eat a granola bar. By the time I'm done with lunch, I've seen two stable hands, someone who looks like a gardener, and a housekeeper from Sweepy Clean—who was on her way out.

Hours go by without any person in sight, so I decide it's time to move. There is an easily accessible location in the barn where I can mount a camera and capture most of the pasture on either side.

I climb to the loft, keeping an eye out, but there are plenty of spaces for hiding. The stacked bales could make a kind of fort. And if I needed to, I could slip between them and the slant of the tin roof, staying well out of sight.

Having had plenty of practice, it won't take me more than five minutes to install a camera. So, covering the barn with good angles pointing out each door and several inside the space too doesn't take very long.

When I'm finished, I climb down.

Straight into *him*.

"Morning," I say, feeling hot and cold flush over my body.

He glances up at my handiwork. "I guess she really wants to keep an eye on things."

I nod, but don't speak, surprised by the mirthless laugh he gives at my non-answer.

"Have a good day, I guess," he says.

I dip my head and turn back to the side of the barn where he entered. Once I'm outside, double back toward my van. I keep checking behind me.

He doesn't seem to notice my odd behavior, but my heart is racing, pounding in my ears. I follow the fence line back to the road, then duck out of sight into the bushes before checking to see if I have been followed.

I wait a while to see if anyone is looking, but there is no one there.

When I finally make it all the way back to the van, I check all my cameras, but everything about the barn seems normal. Matt is still mucking out the stalls, and Gloria is in a lounge chair on the porch, a large sun hat pulled down over her face.

It's another hour before my heart rate goes back to normal.

Matt finishes half the stalls before he goes in for the day.

And even when the house goes quiet, I can't shake the anxiety at nearly having been caught.

The next morning, when Gloria heads out and Matt is back in the barn to do the other half of the stalls, I use the opportunity to install cameras throughout the house. I always pack extras in case something is broken or there are hidden rooms. This time, nothing is damaged, but there is a long, wide hallway down the front of the house with tall windows that looks out on the verdant green pastures.

I try my best not to pick up too much of the outside when I frame the shots.

I finish well before Matt, which is a good thing. It gives me time to get back to the van before he heads in. I head to the back of the house, exit through one of the windows in the sunroom, and follow the fence line back to the road.

It's another couple of hours before Gloria gets home with an armful of designer bags to show for her day's effort.

I test out my setup, watching her put the items away. When she's finished, she pours a glass of white wine, then takes it to the porch with her e-reader.

Matt doesn't come in for dinner. When I check on him, it looks like he spent at least part of the day doing something other than clearing stalls because he still has two left.

Gloria sits outside 'til after dinnertime, but doesn't make any attempt at actually reading. When she finally gets up, she slips on some designer wedges and heads out toward the barn.

The sun has almost set, and the lighting isn't very good.

I put down the granola bar I was eating and turn up the volume on the camera so I can hear if they start talking.

Matt is still in the barn. Earlier, he led a large bay stallion from his stall and tied him on the side of the barn. His work is simple. A load of clean bedding is in the four-by-four, and a wheelbarrow to catch the manure he is chucking out of the stall sits outside the door.

It takes two to three minutes to walk from the house to the big barn. I can tell, even through the grainy lense of the camera, that he is sweating. He has headphones in, and he's humming while he works.

I can hear the tedious cadence of his pitchfork scraping the cement floor of the stable and he shucks the shit across the stall and out the open gate. Each throw is aimed toward the wheelbarrow he's strategically placed.

I imagine what is going to happen before it does, and check the sound again just to make sure I'm not catastrophizing.

Unfortunately, I'm right.

He is a good shot. But it is clear he doesn't hear her coming as she rounds the side of the barn opposite the stud tied at the far end.

She takes a full load of fresh horse shit to the face.

I gasp.

She's so stunned, she doesn't have a chance to move before he chucks the next heap. That's when he notices she is standing there wearing his work.

"Oh my god, Gloria!" he says, taking off his shirt as he goes to her. "I'm so sorry!"

"What the fuck was that?" she asks, wiping at her hair and face.

He pulls his headphones out and sticks them in his pocket. "I'm sorry," he repeats. "I had my headphones in and didn't hear you coming."

She snatches the shirt from his hands and wipes her face. She doesn't hand it back, though. Twisting it around her hand, she dips it into the full wheelbarrow, scooping feces into her palm. She smears it across his face and down his chest.

He doesn't move.

I wait for the explosive rage, but nothing happens.

Even when she does it again, and he wipes it away from his eyes, the anger on his face doesn't boil over.

When she is finished, she stuffs the shirt into the wheelbarrow and turns her back on him, walking back toward the house.

"Fucking idiot," she mutters.

He goes to the spigot and washes his face, then he heads back for his shirt.

TWENTY-SEVEN

Watching through the camera, I wait for him to go in as the sun goes down. But when he tries the doors, they're locked. He knocks a few times and waits.

Gloria's light is on, but there is no movement from her room.

I switch the feed and focus on her to watch what she is doing. She has already showered and changed. She's sitting up in bed with night cream on her face, reading a magazine, and sipping an over-filled glass of red.

When he knocks again, she looks up, but still doesn't move. She is ignoring him.

It isn't cold outside, but his foot is still in the boot. I imagine that he has pain medication and antibiotics to take at the least. From what I can tell, he's got another week before he finishes the course to meet the full ten days. And even if he's off the narcotics, he'll be taking a high dose of ibuprofen.

That doesn't change the fact that staying outside overnight won't be pleasant for his recovery.

He stands back from the door, putting most of his weight on his left foot. After a few more minutes, he steps back and walks around the side of the house toward her window. He stops when he is close enough to see the light on. Then he turns away and walks toward the big barn.

It takes some time before he is close enough that the feed from the barn will pick him up. He looks exhausted. Dirt and horse shit are smeared on his clothes, and there are dark smears that still linger on his face.

I lean back in my seat, trying to figure out what he is doing.

He doesn't turn the light on. He just walks back and forth between the stalls where the horses are stabled on the fresh bedding he's spent the last two days putting down. He goes past them toward the loft, mostly climbing with his arms and left foot. He limps past one of the cameras, but doesn't seem to notice it. Then he curls up in the scattered hay, where it has fallen from the square bales in the loft, using his soiled shirt as a blanket.

I watch for a while. He shifts around on the floor like he's trying to get comfortable on the hard boards and coarse straw that is great for horses, but too rough to be comfortable for sleeping. After a while, he stops moving as much. Then, the only movement is the steady rhythm of his breathing.

That's when I switch back to watching Gloria.

The light in her room is off now, but she is watching something on her tablet. I can't tell exactly what it is, but she seems focused. She uses her fingers to navigate back and forth, sliding it across the bottom of the screen every so often.

It is after ten in the evening now.

I set my monitors to keep an eye on things, pick up the trash from my drinks and protein bars. Then, I change out of my black jeans and into a pair of soft sweats before tumbling into the bed and closing my eyes to sleep.

TWENTY-EIGHT

An alert wakes me, followed by the stabbing fear that I have overslept. It is late in the morning, and the sun is shining through the back window of the van directly into my eyes.

I rub my face and swing my legs to the floor, moving the few feet to the desk and powering on the screens to see what is happening.

Gloria is just getting out of bed.

I watch as she cinches the belt of her satin robe over the matching nightdress and slides on house shoes that make her look like a nineties catalog model for middle-aged women.

She brews a latte and sips it as she moves around the house.

If I hadn't watched her do it, I wouldn't have believed she'd locked her husband out of the house and left him to spend the night in the barn. It makes me nervous for her.

It seems brazen and fearless, like it would anger him beyond belief.

Most of the time, I have the sense of being just in time, but this makes me unsure.

Her eerie calm makes me feel like I am too late. Like something is brewing, and I don't have enough time to prepare.

Even with the cameras up and the time I've spent in the house, I still haven't seen any sign of a child—theirs or someone else's. It seems like it's just the two of them.

The rest of her routine is fairly standard. She takes her pinned-up hair down from curlers, brushes her teeth, and completes a skincare regimen that is extensive and complex.

I lose track after the double cleanse and the eye-lifting serum.

She puts on enough makeup to look like she woke up that way, then applies a generous amount of the standard fragrance that speaks of class but is, by now, more than a little dated. She dresses in white pants and a floral top with matching gold jewelry and a pair of wedges that pull the ensemble together.

After collecting her keys from the dish by the garage door, she heads to her red crossover. I wasn't able to cover every inch of the garage with cameras, but I know which door is going to open.

Matt is nowhere in sight when she backs out of the garage. I check the cameras just to make sure, but he is still curled up in the hayloft.

I can't tell if he is awake or asleep.

She reaches the end of the driveway and pulls into traffic. I already put a tracker on her car, so I'll know when she's on her way back.

I can't decide if I should go back to sleep while I wait to see how he will react. Finally, I decide on an energy drink. Coffee or tea would be rushed, but I need a pick-me-up. I'm half-way done with the can when the camera detects movement.

The grunge has fully set on his clothes and expression, and I can only imagine what he smells like. Bits of straw are stuck in his hair, and the smears of dirt on his clothes have dried to a muddled brown with bits of half-digested grass peppered in.

When he unlocks the front door, I realize something else. He had a key the whole time.

I watch him take it back outside to his hiding place before he goes back into the house.

He takes his boots off before he steps onto the clean floor. Even his socks are dirty, and they leave smudged footprints on the polished tile.

He strips by the door, bundling his clothes up carefully and makes his way to the laundry room where he unwraps the clothes again, and shakes them out over the sink. He puts them in the wash, but doesn't start the load, then goes back upstairs.

I track him through the house as he gathers cleaning supplies, then cleans his path down to the laundry, throws the cleaning rags in with his clothes, adds detergent, and starts the wash.

He goes back upstairs to the primary bathroom and turns on the shower. I don't have a camera in there. It is never the first thing I try.

He hasn't been in the bathroom more than a minute when Gloria's car pulls back into the driveway. I don't switch the audio over, but I pull up the feed side-by-side with the one that watches the bathroom door. She pulls her car into the garage, then three more cars follow her. They stop in the circular drive.

Gloria is already inside the house. She opens the front door and waves as three women step out of their assorted luxury vehicles, wearing brunch attire. Her guests make their way towards her.

I turn the volume up on my headset so my own chewing won't deafen me and open another packet of pistachios.

Matt is still in the shower, but I can't tell if Gloria knows he's back in the primary bedroom.

Gloria welcomes the other women, grabbing several bottles of bubbly from the refrigerator. She goes back for some champagne flutes, then leads them all into the morning room where sunlight streams in through the tall arched windows.

"*Ladies!*" she sings as she sets them down. "Who's ready for a drink?"

Laughter bubbles up, and each of the four women takes a glass.

"Now, I'll be right back."

I move the morning room to a split screen with Gloria so I can follow her through the house.

She still has her heels on. They *click* a staccato tapping as she walks.

It's a big house, and she has a way to go, but I can see the moment she's close enough for him to hear her. He's walking out of the bathroom with a towel wrapped low around his hips.

His jaw tightens, but he keeps his movements nonchalant.

"So now you're going to break into my fucking house," she says.

That's her greeting.

"Gloria, I needed a shower. And I had to clean my boot, change the bandage, and take my antibiotics. I was late taking the dose, and my foot fucking hurts." He sounds more tired than anything.

"Now you're going to curse at me?"

"I wasn't—I didn't—I'm just tired. I did not sleep well."

"Well, you weren't supposed to, Matt. That's what happens when you don't pay attention to what you're doing."

"Right. So I piss you off, and then I have to sleep in shit and filth and I'm not allowed to follow basic instructions from a doctor so I don't get an infection from the shard they pulled out of my foot? From the glass that you threw at me?"

"Oh, please," she scoffs. "Always so dramatic. It was a scratch."

"You *broke* my foot. I had a cut that needed seventeen stitches, Gloria. That is not a scratch."

What the fuck, Gloria? I sit up in my chair and turn the volume up a little even though they are already talking pretty loudly. That's a hell of an accident, if that's what she wants to sell it as.

"Look, I understand that you want to fight about this, but I honestly don't have the time right now. I have company. Things will go a lot better for you after they leave if you do what I need you to do."

"Yeah," he mutters, "what's that?"

Anger is coming off of him in waves so palpable that I can feel it through the screens.

I glance over at the women in the morning room to see they are still talking and laughing and pouring another round. They have no idea what's happening at the other end of the house.

And Gloria continues speaking in a low, menacing tone.

"You're going to come out and wait on me and my friends," she says. "You're going to look sexy and treat me like a queen. You're going to treat them like the fucking ladies of my court, and you're going to make us a nice Southern breakfast with full hospitality."

Her commands keep coming. "You're going to look like my fucking pool boy while you do it, and show them exactly what it is that my money has bought me. You're going to do it with a fucking smile. You can put some underwear on and leave it at that. I don't want them to have to imagine how good I have it. They need to *see* it."

She closes the bedroom door when she heads back toward the morning room. Her heels clicking like a metronome as she walks, she wipes her hands on her skirt.

I minimize the screen when Matt reaches for his towel and switch my focus back to Gloria and the girls.

TWENTY-NINE

When he walks into the kitchen, he's wearing a polo, khaki shorts, and loafers. And his wedding ring is not on the fourth finger of his left hand.

He starts the grits first, then dices the onion and peppers. He already has cubed potatoes soaking in cold water in the fridge. He takes out the eggs and shreds some cheese, then starts bacon and sausage in separate cast-iron pans. He sets the table in the breakfast room.

The meat is just starting to sizzle.

He cracks the eggs and whisks them in a bowl with a little milk, salt, pepper, and a spice blend.

The way he moves in the kitchen reminds me of Corrin. I hope she's doing okay. I want to check and make sure the shock of everything wasn't too much, that she's found a good therapist, and has started healing.

It occurs to me that whenever my target is cooking I'm usually starving and eating a cold cereal bar or some other garbage.

I would kill for a hot meal. I chuckle at my own joke.

He stirs the grits.

I take another bite of my granola bar.

He takes the bacon and sausage out of their respective pans and drains off some of the grease. The potatoes go into the sausage skillet.

Taking an assortment of berries from the fridge, he places them in a salad spinner and washes them, then spins away the water before putting them in decorative bowls. Those go on the table, then three large carafes of juice, red, pink—probably grapefruit, and orange.

My guess for the red is cranberry, but I can't be sure.

He stirs the potatoes and the grits, then mixes the eggs and adds onions and peppers before combining it in the pan with bacon fat. The contents hiss and bubble, prompting him to turn down the flame on the gas range.

I'm so focused on his cooking, I don't notice Gloria in the corner of the frame until he jumps.

"Jesus," he says, picking up the wooden spoon he dropped. "You startled me."

Gloria arches a perfectly-plucked, rail-thin brow. "Where's your wedding ring?"

Matt looks at his hand, and his brow furrows. "I guess I left it on the tray in the bathroom." He shrugs and turns back to the stove, stirring eggs, potatoes, and grits again. He takes the eggs off the stove first, then the grits, placing them on a folded towel near the stove. Then he grabs a serving bowl and scrapes the potatoes into it.

Gloria grabs a potholder so she doesn't burn herself on the metal handles. She takes the pot of grits off the counter and tosses it at him, letting the contents slop out onto him, then flinging the cast iron for good measure.

I gasp.

"*Jesus fucking Christ!*" he shouts.

The cookware hits him in the stomach, steaming grits slop down his arms. A few spots speckle his cheek and chin. The pot clangs as it hits his booted foot, and some of the dregs splash onto his shins.

"*What the fuck, Gloria?* What the actual fuck?"

He puts the pan he's holding on a cold stove burner.

The laughter from the morning room stops, and one of the braver ladies heads toward the kitchen.

Two of the others linger in the hallway, and the third carries the bottles of wine into the breakfast room.

"Is everything okay?" the blonde woman asks.

"It's fine, Marissa. Matt and I were just discussing how the next time I ask him to do something, I expect it to be done."

Marissa raises her eyebrows, but doesn't say anything. She just stands in the doorway with a face that might look worried if it still had the ability to form expressions.

Matt turns the cold water on in the sink and wipes away the grits with a towel. His skin is blotchy and red, but welts haven't started to form yet.

He opens the freezer and reaches for some ice.

"No, wait, not like that," Marissa says, stepping around the mess of grits and the just-visible crack in the tile floor where the cast-iron pot landed, "ice will make it worse." She turns the faucet handle and sticks her hand into the stream. "There, you actually want the water to be cool, not cold."

Gloria stands looking on, the potholder still in her hand.

"Are you okay?" Marissa asks, turning to Gloria.

"Yes—yes, I just thought," Gloria stammers, "I thought he was going to…"

Marissa raises her eyebrows but doesn't say anything like she doesn't quite believe Gloria's change of tone.

Matt pulls his shirt off, revealing toned abs and a patchwork of red burns across his tattooed skin. He rinses the towel in the stream of cool water from the sink and wipes grits off his legs too.

Those burns don't look as bad as the ones on his arms.

Matt hisses, putting his hands back into the stream of water and letting it run over his arms.

Marissa takes the potholder from Gloria and picks the pot up off the floor, placing it on the mat on the counter, then she grabs some paper towels and wipes the rest of it off the floor and throws away the wad of towels.

She washes her hands when she is finished, then turns to Gloria. "I can take the rest of the food into the breakfast room and get us started if you like, or we can all go."

"Thank you," Gloria says, squeezing Marissa's arm. "I'd like it if you'd stay. I'll be along in a minute if you can get brunch started."

Marissa nods, then gathers the rest of the items on a tray and heads to the other room. She is back in a moment to get the rest of the food, then she is gone again. She doesn't look back when she leaves the second time.

Matt is still leaning against the sink, running water over his arms.

Gloria stalks toward him. She slides her hands down his chest to the front of his pants, unfastening the button and letting the stained shorts drop around his feet. She reaches her hand into his underwear.

The look on his face says she's tightened her grasp, and when she steps in closer, he almost doubles over.

Her taloned French manicure digs into his chin, her hand drawing his face down to her eye-level. Her lips are close to his, nearly brushing his cheek when she speaks.

Her voice is too low for me to hear what she is saying.

I reach over to the audio and manually adjust it, trying to pick up her words.

"…and we'll talk about this tonight." She releases him and leaves the kitchen, heading down the hall toward her bedroom.

Matt sinks to the floor curled in a ball, panting, his shorts still bunched around his ankles, his cheek pressed against the floor.

A light flipping on in another frame draws my attention back to Gloria. She is in the office, placing some folders from her bag into the wall safe. She closes it and locks it.

I grab a scrap of paper and write the combination before I forget. I want to know what she's selling, and what she's bought.

The Creepy multi-level-marketing vibes are throwing me off.

The rest of the morning seems uneventful, and the ladies enjoy their brunch.

Matt spends the rest of the day in and out of a cold bath and applying a numbing antiseptic spray between rounds of hydrotherapy.

Gloria never checks on him.

For the first time, I'm thinking about what it will be like to kill a woman. I always thought I was doing this because of my mother, to help people like her. It just never occurred to me that it might be a woman abusing and taking advantage of someone. It's hard to imagine a woman who doesn't understand the fear of someone who will do anything to get what they want.

But I guess Gloria has never lived through that. Or if she has, it's turned her bitter and cold, and now she doesn't give a shit about anyone else.

I rest during the day as best I can, trying to keep an eye on things, but it's shaping up to be a long one. Something about their fight feels unfinished, and I'm still waiting for the other shoe to drop.

Gloria is in bed with a sheet mask on her face when he comes in from another bath. He's spraying more of the lidocaine on when she reaches into her nightstand and pulls out a revolver. She pulls back the hammer. It makes an audible click.

She doesn't speak.

He is frozen, the can of spray curled in his fist.

"Gloria," he asks, "what are you doing?"

She pulls the trigger.

He flinches. Now he is silent.

"Do you think it's fun for me when I don't know what you're going to do? Have no idea how you're going to act? And then you embarrass me in front of my friends?"

"Gloria, I don't know what you mean. I didn't—"

"See, the thing is, it doesn't make it any better that you don't know what you did wrong." She pulls the trigger again.

Another hollow click fills the space between them.

"Jesus, Lo," he says, taking half a step toward her.

"Don't."

He stills, his gaze trained on her hand, tracking each movement as she pulls back the hammer again.

"You stay there. Just listen," she says.

THIRTY

He cuffs himself to the bed frame when she tells him to, then takes a seat on the edge of the mattress, twisting to the side at an awkward angle. I can tell he's trying not to pull too hard against the restraints.

"Look at me."

He turns his face to her.

"You've been so clever, sneaky like a snake." She slaps him hard across the cheek, her long nails leaving red scratches. "See what you made me do?"

He keeps his face toward from her, but he averts his eyes as she holds up her palm, pinked by the force of striking his face.

If he kicked out with his feet, hit her in the stomach, I know he could hurt her. He doesn't. I know he won't. If he were going to fight back, he would have already.

Gloria disappears into the bathroom. When she comes back, she has changed into a black latex bodysuit and matching boots, and she has a pair of scissors in hand. I clench my teeth, watching to see what she's going to do.

Even as a woman of violence, there are some things that make me cringe, at least when they're happening to people who don't deserve it.

But she doesn't cut him or stab him with them. Instead, she cuts away his clothes, leaving him more vulnerable than before, revealing the tattoos that cover his arms and chest. Somehow, that seems worse. He has some on his legs too, and in between the ink, I can see the patchy red of burns from earlier today.

He doesn't complain.

"So," she says, "you and Marissa."

His eyes go wide with surprise, but it must be because the accusation is so absurd.

I've been watching. There's been nothing like that.

She runs a fingernail over one of the burns, and he hisses in pain.

A smile twists her lips.

I turn the volume up on my headset when she continues speaking.

"God, you were so young and beautiful when I got you, all that perfect bronze skin, and you had to go and mark it up. I don't think you ever consider what I want or how I feel anymore. You used to worship the ground I walked on. I think I liked you better when you were fifteen." She favors him with a nasty, malicious smile. "I think sometimes you forget that you're replaceable. I could have another, younger you in a few days. I could start over with him."

She pushes the chair from the corner of the room toward him, then goes to the walk-in closet. I can't see what she does in there, but she comes back with a box and places it on the other side of the king-size bed.

"Maybe you and I just start over together, and I can remind you what it is you fell in love with in the beginning. Maybe I should remind you why *you* obey *me*." She opens the chest and takes out a leather whip and hits him with it.

There isn't any preamble. Just a snake-like motion that catches him on the side of the head and wraps around from behind.

"Get on your knees."

He does.

The handcuffs stretch his arms across the bed from the headboard to the edge of the bed where he's kneeling.

It was never him.

This isn't even what I was expecting. I was so sure he had found some way to take advantage of her. I can't help feeling like I've let him down. I judged the situation before I knew what was happening, and maybe I missed a red flag. I let things go further than I should have because I was waiting for him to hurt her. Now I'm sitting with him in this…thing, and I don't feel like I have the right to because I wasn't here for him. Not at first.

I knew that it was possible that she was aggressive toward him—maybe reactive—I did, but I've never seen a woman do this before. There were fights and arguments, but now I'm frightened for him. I'm scared that it's too late because I don't know how far she's willing to take this. Everything else I've seen has been sparked by a moment of rage, but this is a storm that's been brewing. She's been planning this, and I can't tell if she's ready to "trade" him in as she mentioned or try to "remind" him.

The chest is filled with whips, cuffs, chains, smaller boxes and bags.

Gloria takes the whip to his back and the backs of his legs.

He's silent the whole time, but I can see the red marks from the repeated strikes in the same place.

Whatever she's done in the past, she hasn't left permanent scars. It seems she likes pretty things, and while bruises fade, cuts and scars have not been on the menu. Aside from the new one on his foot.

If she changes her mind, I'm pretty sure he's going to die.

Gloria fastens a spreader bar between his ankles, then she puts a pair of cuffs on his hands that ends with a leather lead.

She guides him from her bedroom, down the hall and out the front door to the small—what I had mistaken for a tack room–stable near the front of the house. His walk is awkward and slow, so it takes them a while.

When she finishes arranging him, he is tied to a sawhorse, draped over a saddle that is mounted on the spine of it, like it is the back of an animal. His legs are spread and tied to the feet of the sawhorse on one side, and his hands bound to the legs on the other. She covers his face with blinders. They look like the kind a pair of draft horses would wear while working.

She checks to make sure his bindings are secure. Then she opens a small padlock that holds a shelf closed against the wall. When she pulls it down, it reveals a work table with more of her tools above it. She has a large assortment of whips, ropes, chains, clamps, dildos, straps, and other items too small for me to identify on screen.

She takes things a step further by placing a bit with a ball gag in his mouth.

She pulls a riding crop from the wall, teases it across his arms to one of the red welts from the burns and snaps it hard.

He groans around the bit in his mouth. Gloria tugs at the reins in a way that would rile even the best-tempered horse.

She whips him again, then turns on a bright stage light, directing the beam at him.

When she turns on a camera I hadn't noticed before, I realize it's not one of mine.

Her black boots are waterproof rubber. They protect her from the pine wood chip bedding on the floor.

She turns the faucet on and picks up the hose that was coiled on the wall rack, then aims the jet stream at him, hosing him down in cold water. She starts with his face, blasting the jet directly at his mouth, nose, and eyes, then she moves to the back of his head, not missing his ears. She moves the stream over his back and sides, getting under his arms, then working her way up under his chin and down what is exposed of his chest, stomach and legs.

When she's finished, she sprays down his glutes and between his thighs. She starts again. This time, she holds the stream over his face for a long time.

He gasps for air when she eventually directs the stream away from his face.

She pauses long enough for him to catch his breath, then she starts again with the whip, working her way over his body the same way she did with the hose. Only this time, she seems to focus exclusively on where she burned him before.

He had been silent the first time, but the grunts of pain grow louder as she alternates between whipping and the cold.

I glance at the clock. It is already *9:30*.

She has been at it for nearly a half hour. He looks exhausted. She looks like she is just getting started.

There isn't any way I can stop this.

She's facing the door, with the camera behind her.

If she's streaming this, I don't know how many people would see me or where they might be. If she sees me, there are any number of makeshift weapons at her disposal, and I don't know what she would do to Matt if I barged in.

She's guilty. That much is obvious, so I will do what needs to be done. But as things stand, there would be no clean getaway for me. I'd be relying on him as a witness and hoping to high heaven he doesn't say anything about my being here. And to top it all off, she already has a hostage.

He is braver than I am, and I can't help thinking that is the worst part—he's never had a choice. There isn't anything she wants. There's no way he can convince her to stop.

It isn't about that for her.

She wants to break him. It is her way of making sure he knows that any kindness she might show him is a gift and she can take it away at any point in time.

His eyes are bloodshot, but it is difficult to tell if it is from the cold water or tears. Maybe it's both.

I'm relieved when she turns the hose off at the spigot.

When she reaches for a bristle brush, I realize I may have been too optimistic in hoping she was done.

She starts with his hands, rubbing him down like an animal. Her strokes are rough over his arms regardless of the welts, burns, and bruises that are purpling beneath his skin. She hasn't bothered to towel him down either, and I try not to imagine what the cold, wet chafing feels like.

She adjusts the sawhorse with a saddle fixed to it. The wet leather grabs his skin as she tightens the shackles from his left arm and leg, pulling him forward more. She then adjusts the others so he is more bent over the saddle like he's in a fireman carry. She selects the next implement from the wall and places it on the table, then she goes back for the hose.

My stomach churns.

She turns the mount so the camera has a better angle, then takes the hose, turns the jet back on and aims it up against his anus.

When she turns the water on, he gasps.

THIRTY-ONE

I've seen a lot of things, done a lot of things, but most don't make me recoil like this. Not just because I don't like shit and being cold, but what's happening to him is my fault.

Gloria leaves the hose on for a long time, keeping the nozzle pressed against him, even when he twists and tries to get away. When she turns the hose off, the jet reverses, his bowels convulsively expelling water and shit in a torrent.

I know frigid water like that can cause cramping.

When the stream slows, she places the hose against him again and squeezes the trigger on the nozzle. It's the colonic from hell. If I had to guess, this isn't the first time she's done this.

I think I know what she's getting him ready for.

The urge to get out of the van is so strong. But there isn't a way for me to really help him. Now I feel like I'm slipping. This isn't the first time I've missed something recently, and I'm beginning to think the distractions I've been dealing with are clouding my judgement. And that's dangerous.

I look at the network again. It doesn't look like that camera is on their home Wi-Fi. The only other signal it could be connected to is weaker, and further away unless the camera is hardwired. I make a note on my scratchpad to dig into it later. Right now, Matt needs me.

She stops with the hose when the water from his bowels comes out clear, and maybe I've been watching her long enough to know now, but I have a sinking feeling things are about to get worse.

I'm right.

They get really bad.

Gloria takes down one of the strap-ons from the wall, fastening it to her body. Maybe it would have been a small mercy if she lubed it up, but I can see where she's going with it and there's none in sight.

It's girthy.

She turns the sawhorse again, checking to make sure the camera has a good angle, like she knows exactly where things need to be.

Without warming him up in any way, she pushes into him.

He doesn't scream. The sound he makes is a low, deep intake of breath, like when you can't breathe in or properly fill your lungs with air. The theme that keeps coming up with her is the way there's no definable end. He's not getting off on it, and neither is she. At least at the moment.

Not all abusers do, but I can't understand her point. Why she chose the means she did. The goal is always suffering and control. But what makes her feel like she's gotten her point across? That's what I can't figure out.

Something about this makes me more conflicted than the others, like it's easier for me to understand the pain women experience. Maybe because it's not just dismissed by everyone. The thing I hate is that while people recognize that women are the victims the majority of the time, people don't do anything about it. But when it's a boy or a man, people don't even acknowledge it. They excuse it completely. There's this idea that whenever a woman who is older than a boy takes advantage of him, he is somehow lucky and it makes his peers jealous. So often, they laugh it off, give him an attaboy, and offer to buy him a beer.

How's he supposed to talk about that?

She reaches around and starts to jerk him off while she's thrusting into him. It takes a while before he responds at all, but she is persistent, moving torturously slow. She isn't going to stop 'til she gets him off and humiliates him all at the same time.

It's so uncomfortable because his arousal is a mechanical function, a biological response to physical contact that has nothing to do with what his brain wants. It's disconcerting that it happens to a lot of victims. I know logically this is where so much shame comes from.

It's where people assume that just because the person had an orgasm, it wasn't *rape.*

People fucking suck.

The thing is, he could have hurt her. She would have called him a wife-beater and told everyone what he did.

Or he could do what he did. Handcuff himself to a bed and be tortured in a way of her choosing.

After he finally ejaculates, she bends over him, whispering against his back.

He is silent, or at least I can't hear what he says, and with the camera angle, if he answers, I can't read his lips.

When she is done, she leaves him like that.

Naked and tied to the sawhorse.

THIRTY-TWO

He is so quiet. Anxiety settles in my stomach. I sit still for a while, thinking, staring at the screen. He isn't moving. I know she hasn't killed him. That's something I've never seen. A victim die, someone I was trying to save. I didn't want today to be the first time that happened. I look closer, zoom in.

He is moving. His shoulders are shaking. He's crying.

Even as I try to remind myself of the reasons I can't go in, guilt screams in my ear. Would it really be the worst thing if I got caught? If he didn't have to suffer this because, overall, what does my life matter compared to misery like that?

But it's not just my future. I know that's what Percilla would say. This is when she would remind me of all the other people in the world who need my help. Girls like Olivia, men like Matt, and yes, women like my mother and Corrin. I have to stick to the plan because it keeps me safe.

It keeps *all* of us safe.

But there is no way I can stay for this. I don't deserve to be the one comforting him, sharing his pain. I fucked this one up. *Bad.*

I cut the feed and focus on Gloria. She is almost back to the house, the porch light showing a path from the tack room to the front step with its white rocking chairs and black shutters. It is bright enough that she doesn't need a flashlight. She hasn't even bothered to lock the door. It is strange how their home in the city was so secure and this one is not even locked, like they never worry about what happens here.

Most likely, because they don't seem to spend a lot of time here. Even with the few horses they have, it looks like some caretaker comes in when they are away. But no employees have stayed into the afternoon since the first day I followed them home. If the routine stays the same, someone should be here to work on the perfectly manicured lawn tomorrow morning, and Matt will be able to call for help. Or maybe, someone will look for Gloria, wanting to get paid. They'll be sure to look for Matt once they discover her body.

I leave the feed of Gloria pulled up on my monitor so I can keep an eye on it, then I lay a large heavy-duty black trash bag out on my bed and empty the contents of my backpack onto it. When I know the bag is empty, I spread out my tools to make sure I'm taking what I need. I put an extra handcuff key up my sleeve in addition to the one I keep around my neck. They aren't universal, but the ones I carry are common enough.

My standard length of rope, several pairs of gloves, extra shoe covers, more trash bags, extra knives, handcuffs and a few more keys (they get lost easily and if a spare is great a few more is even better), a first-aid kit (that's for me, I don't usually need it, but you know what they say about needing and not having). I have a big flashlight too, sturdy enough that I can hit someone with it, and still have it fulfil lits primary function. A black light, lock picks, a box cutter, laser pointer, duct tape, a folding knife, and some spare thumb drives.

I don't usually take anything from the house that I didn't bring with me when I came in, but I'd rather be prepared if I need to take something this time, especially with the files. I check the lining of my backpack's front pocket, too. I've turned it into a bit of a booster bag. Once I'm sure it's intact, I organize everything in the pack, putting the first-aid kit at the bottom of the main compartment, the hundred feet of static line and trash bags on top where they're accessible. I put the gloves and shoe covers in the mesh side pockets where I can get to them easily without digging in the whole bag.

Before I go, I check the cameras again, and I can see Gloria has been even worse than I had thought. I have to hurry.

I know exactly what I'm going to do to her.

There's also one thing they have here that I'm going to use. It's in the real tack room that is actually for horses, not the one that is wired for the camera.

I test it quickly to make sure it is working, then I carefully put it in my bag and head for the house.

The light in the torture room is on, but the door is closed.

THIRTY-THREE

Matt is still tied up in the room of horrors. But it's also the only way I know he'll be safe, at least from people thinking he's the one who murdered her. Then I'll just have to wait around 'til someone finds him. Hopefully, it's one of the farm hands. Then they can go in to the house and find Gloria's dead body together.

Usually, with women, there's a bit of wiggle room. People don't expect this kind of thing from us. I'll be in the clear. But with Gloria's money, there's no chance investigators won't suspect Matt.

There's a part of me that is uneasy, frightened, even.

I've never killed a woman before. Just the idea of it feels unnatural to me. The way I kill usually is so intuitive I'm not used to having to think about it. But I saw what she did. If she were a man, I never would have hesitated.

This is getting messy. It's counter to what I usually let myself think, but there is a part of me that has to find joy in the work that I do. I need to be able to like my job or I'll burn out. Even if the parts I love are the people I've saved, I have to keep the spark alive.

At first, it is hard to decide how to do this one.

Gloria is worse to Matt than most people are to animals, and to end her the same way animals are slaughtered is also too kind. But I don't know if I have the stomach to torture her, to truly make the suffering equitable to what she's inflicted. It's difficult because, overall, I like to think the pain is the lesson and the balance the universe needs. But the death is because, above everything else, people don't learn. They'll always go back to a behavior they think they got away with.

I know that's what Gloria believes. That she is free.

But that is an illusion.

Once I'm safely inside the house and I don't have to worry about looking like a highlighter in the pitch black yard, I unzip the pack, take out the painter's suit, and pull it on over my black clothes.

I know exactly where she's headed.

Gloria turns out the lights as she moves through the house. I follow her to her room and wait while she gets ready for sleep. The door to her bedroom is open, and she's just like I saw her last. Her robe is on, but it's open, and she's watching the TV.

It's a recording of her and Matt from years ago.

I can tell from how young he looks.

She has a vibrator in one hand and she's got the TV remote in the other, turning up the volume.

Her cell is on the nightstand, charging. I grab it as I step into the room and push it into my back pocket.

Once she's secured, I'll turn it off.

She gives a little scream when I take the phone, the lubed-up toy flying out of her hand as she jumps up and sweeps the robe around her naked body.

I realize the outfit she's wearing is the same one on the TV screen.

"Who are you and what do you want?" she asks, already backing away. She glances down to tie her robe closed.

I take a step forward as she does.

"Get out of my house!" She moves back toward the window, glancing around frantically.

I've already got her phone, and the only thing behind her is a large window with a view of the pitch-black backyard.

She lunges for the nightstand. I know that's where she keeps the gun, but I step forward, grasping her by the hair. A chunk of it comes out in my hand. It must be about time for her to get her extensions redone. She stumbles onto her hands and knees.

I grab her again before she can get any further and tie her hands behind her back. She kicks out at me as I get them in place, and she flips onto her back. She's stronger than she looks, but not stronger than I am. I drag her up onto the bed and secure her to the frame, the same way she had Matt anchored in the barn.

"Now," I say, taking the seat she'd scooted closer to the bed, "let's have a little chat. Just us girls." With my gloved hand, I grab the remote from the bed beside her and turn the volume down. I leave the video playing. I don't want her to hide from what she's done to him. I want investigators to see what kind of person she was.

"Who the fuck are you?"

"Who I am is not important. It's why I'm here that you should be worrying about."

"Fine. Why are you here?"

"Your husband," I say, gesturing toward the TV. "How old was he when you bought him?"

I'm taking a guess, but I think it's a pretty good one. I can't find any record of Matt's family. Just Gloria. That's all he's got.

She looks genuinely surprised.

"Did you have him before he was fifteen, or is that just when you started messing with him?" The answer isn't all that important. She's going to end up the same regardless of what she says, but I am curious.

"Why do you care?" She asks, "Do you want one? I can get you a new boy, or you can have him." She nods toward the shed. "It's time for me to trade up, anyway. He's getting kind of old for me."

I raise my brow. So I wasn't a moment too soon. "What were you going to do with him? Murder him?"

"Don't be ridiculous. *I* wasn't going to do anything. There are people for that."

"Is it expensive? I don't really know anything about this kind of arrangement. I mean, when I kill people, I do it for free."

Her face goes white.

"Listen, Gloria, I get it," I lean back in the chair. "Men are difficult. But that is never going to justify taking advantage of and abusing a child. Because let's be perfectly clear, setting aside the fact that you *bought* a person, he was a *child*. He wasn't a man, but a boy. And you took him, isolated him, and abused him."

"Well, did you leave him in the barn?" Her tone is sarcastic when she asks, not because she cares, but because she's trying to drag me down to her level.

"I did. I don't want them to think what I do to you was done by him. Luckily, you've given him the perfect alibi." I smile. "Now, Gloria, where should we start?"

After I open a trash bag and place it on the floor, ready for use, I'm ready to begin.

THIRTY-FOUR

I go into her closet and look for the box I saw her take out earlier. Her space is well-organized. The case is easy to find, placed on a middle shelf near her shoes. I bring it out and place it on the bed beside her. When I push the metal buttons on either side, the latches pop open, making a loud clicking sound.

Gloria flinches.

"It's different when you're on the receiving end, isn't it?" I ask. "You know, the part I found especially hard to watch was the rape. You did a lot more torture than some of the others I've dealt with. I'm not sure if that was for you or your audience. I could probably be persuaded to go a little easier on you if you tell me who the recordings are for. I can see that the torture wasn't your favorite part. That's not what gets you off, right?"

She doesn't answer. I run my gloved hands over the items in the kit, nipple clamps, tassels, whips, things she uses on him however she pleases. She never thought of how those things would feel to others.

"Tell me, what's your least favorite thing in this box?"

I watch her face as I trace my hand over the assorted ropes, bindings, and chains, looking for a tell.

She purses her lips, determined not to answer any of my questions.

"It's okay, you don't have to tell me." I pick up some rope first.

Her face remains impassive.

I move to the nipple clamps, but she doesn't seem to care.

She doesn't seem to like the pegging kit. That's a hard limit for me, but it does give me some inspiration. I imagine she also doesn't like the bar that she used on Matt.

Too bad it's still outside with him.

It doesn't seem like she uses any of the chastity restraints or the ball cages, which in her case, wouldn't do any good.

I think I'll keep it simple.

The clamps go back in the box, and I take the whip she seemed to favor using on Matt. I run the tassels over my palm and give it a test flick. It would be very painful if used over burns. I light the red candle that sits on her dressing table. The scent says bergamot and jasmine. I lay the whip at the foot of the bed, then take the rope from my bag and cut another length to tie her legs with, straight and still, the way she tied Matt in the tack room.

"Does any of this feel familiar?" I ask her. "Like maybe you've been here before?"

"If you're into me, you could at least take me to dinner first," she says. "I know mommy issues when I see them."

"That's really funny, Gloria, because honestly, you have no idea," I grin when I say it, really selling her what she wants to believe.

That's the thing about not knowing my family. When someone says something terrible about them, I don't feel anything. But knowing what I know now, with Gloria, I'm finding that I want to hurt her. I want her to feel the pain I know she's caused others.

I believe I can draw blood from a stone and make this cold, unfeeling bitch pay for what she's done.

I'm not just going to torture her because she deserves it. I'm going to break her because I want to do it.

I turn my back to her and compose myself. For the first time in my life, I am afraid of who I am becoming.

The clock reads *11:37*.

"We have plenty of time, but I don't feel like cooking grits. Besides, I don't want to leave you by yourself. You might get bored or lonely. Also, when I work, I like to think of it in terms of checks and balances. For example, you've had Matt here for what, ten years? And during that time you've done untold horrors to him. So while I can't keep you alive for ten years—because nobody has time for that—you should still get a solid taste of what you put him through."

I pick up the dildo that's been flopping around on the floor.

"Oh, you dropped this." I press the buttons on the side, cycling between the rhythms and speeds, then settle on the fastest one. "Let me put it back for you."

It's already got some lube on it so when I shove it in her anus, I don't have to fight it too hard. She gasps and shudders, the arrogant expression falling from her face.

"No, that wasn't…"

She's still putting it together. I imagine it's hard to think with a wad of silicone buzzing violently in your rectum.

"Yeah," I answer, "that didn't have a flared base. Oops. I guess it's gone, but not forgotten. Am I right?"

I laugh at my own joke.

"I noticed that was something Matt didn't seem to like. When you were putting stuff in his anus without permission. So, now that we've tried that, how do you feel?" I wait for her answer.

Her face is contorted in an expression that isn't pleasure or pain, but a discomfort that walks a very fine line between the two.

I'm sure I can find a way to tip it over to the side of agony very easily. Pacing around the room, I check on the burning wick. A watched candle never turns into enough melted wax to torture someone.

I use the box cutter to shred her robe away instead of untying her hands. There's a moment when her eyes brighten with terror and she thinks I'm going to slice into her. I almost do—it's the most emotion I've seen out of her since I started this. The look fades as I fold the blade away and stow it in my pocket. Maybe later.

She starts to cry when I use the blade to remove the extensions from her hair, leaving a messy patchwork behind.

I toss the ragged clumps onto the floor. I rip away her fake lashes too, some of the real ones coming away at the root where the others are sewn in.

"Gloria," I say as I continue my work, "I want you to understand that this isn't about how you look." I gesture at the beautification I've already stripped away. "These are just symptoms of the real problem. You don't like yourself. You're so afraid that he's going to find an age-appropriate partner. Someone he chooses. And that he will get on with the life he deserves while you'll be here aging and alone with who you really are inside."

I reach into her case and pull out some pliers and place them on the nightstand where they'll be easy to reach for. "What are these for?"

She eyes them, but doesn't answer.

"All the stuff you put on the outside just hides the nastiness in your soul." I pull the knife from my pocket and cut her.

She screams, tries to pull away.

I slice again, redefining the frown lines on her forehead and the ones that ring her mouth. Blood runs down her face.

"These could have been laugh lines. And honestly if they were, I probably wouldn't be here, but it's like I said, you've tried to hide something evil. But it keeps oozing through your skin. And I can't decide if you're worse than a man because as a woman, I'm sure you know exactly what it feels like to be on the other end of this."

When she stops screaming and her mewling has settled to whimpers, I take the pliers and rip away a manicured nail.

Her scream is so loud, I'm glad the houses are so far apart here.

"You told Matt that you hated his tattoos. What if he doesn't like your nails? Aren't you marking up your body, too?" I rip away another and another, not giving her time to recover between each one.

Even for me, this is nasty and makes my stomach turn. But it has to be done.

When her fingers are capped with bleeding nubs, I push her head back, my gloved palm smearing across the cuts on her forehead so I can look into her mouth.

"Are the teeth real?"

"Yes!" she shrieks. "Oh god, yes, they're mine! What the fuck is wrong with you?"

I shrug. "That's probably for the best. Tooth extractions are a lot of work."

Moving on, I probe one breast in a clinical way. It's fake.

Her eyes flare when I swap out the pliers for the box cutter again.

I follow the line under each one where the doctor meticulously cut and stitched, tuning out the scream as I follow the thin whitened skin.

"Your surgeon did a good job. The scar was so faint, it was difficult to follow."

The implant is on top of the muscle. Subglandular is much more convenient for unprofessional removal.

She whimpers.

"I can't decide if I've done this in the right order or not. If you're already in too much pain to feel what I'm going to do next, that would be a shame."

Her eyes roll around to focus on me.

She looks dazed, and maybe even a little more exhausted than Matt was.

I smile at her.

She begins to cry harder.

I check the candle. There's a pool of bright red liquid. It's finally melted enough. I blow out the flame and pour it over her body. "I don't think most people know this, but by now you've realized that the wax they use for fun isn't the same kind of wax they use in candles."

Tears roll down her face, and air hisses between her teeth, but she doesn't say anything.

"Is the vibrator still going?" I ask, watching the wax turn from glistening red to a soft matte finish.

"Please," she gasps. "Get it out, or take me to a hospital. I can't stand it!"

I chuckle. "No, Gloria, we both know I'm not going to do that. Now hold still. I'm going to get this wax off your skin now that it's cool. I don't want to cut you." I pause. Frown. "Well, I don't want to do it again. Not yet."

I lean over her with the box cutter, using the blade to peel the cooled wax away. I'm not particularly careful and when she winces in pain, I'm not bothered.

She looks like a polka dot patchwork when I'm finished, red burns starting to brighten on her sun-tanned skin. "It's not as good as the grits, but it gives the general idea, don't you think?"

"How do you know about the grits?" she asks, her eyes going wide with surprise.

"I've been watching you for a little while now," I confess. "I wonder what your friends would think if they knew you threw that pot at him on purpose."

She flicks her fingers in dismissal. The ropes prevent her from moving further and jerk against the wooden headboard.

I take the whip in hand and lash it at one of the burns and scars on her body.

She screams.

It feels a bit dramatic, like she's putting on a show, hoping it will placate me. I hit harder the next time, aiming for one of the larger welts on her abdomen. This time when she writhes, I'm more convinced. But I think it's the vibrator that's lost somewhere in her intestines. I'm sure, with a pinch in the right place, it would be pure anguish. I hit her again.

I did a good job of spreading the wax around, so there are plenty of targets, but I focus on the ones across her breasts and abdomen because they make her shy away more, and the shifting is what really causes pain.

I lash her thighs a bit, too, where the skin is particularly thin.

I think it's worse for her since aging makes it even thinner. When I hit a welt on her inner thigh, she nearly curls into a ball, but the rope bindings stop her.

She tries to catch her breath, but only ends up wheezing and hyperventilating. Now it's definitely not in pleasure. She's fallen over the thin line to the side of pure pain, and I think the lost object may be doing some real damage, though I'm not exactly sure how bad it could be. The object has no sharp edges.

"Something is—" she says, struggling to breathe. "I think something is really wrong."

"Well, I should hope so," I answer. "Otherwise, I've not been doing a very good job."

But she's gone pale.

I realize I've overlooked something about her face, even where I've emphasized the lines that she's tried desperately to hide. I lean forward, examining her hairline, brushing the edges forward as I search for the telltale scar.

She's definitely had a facelift.

I follow the line around her face, in front of her ears, temples and down under the side of her jaw to remove jowls. From what I can tell, she's had a pretrichial brow lift, temporal lift, and a lower rhytidectomy. Those have to go.

There's true terror in her eyes when I pick up the box cutter this time. A guttural scream rips from her lungs as I start the incision, following the surgical scars and connecting the gaps between them from each of the surgeries.

Once I've completed the outline of her face, I use the pliers to grasp the skin and start to work the blade of the box cutter under the flap of skin, separating it from the tissue underneath. I'm not too concerned about how deep I go. It will just be easier if I get the skin off in one piece. I need it to be thick enough that I can get a solid grip closer to the eyes, nose, and mouth. I'm not worried about the time since I don't have to put everything back where I found it.

Gloria thrashes her limbs against me, but I can tell she's scared to move her face too much, afraid that I'll cut even deeper. I'm surprised she hasn't passed out, but I can tell she's going into shock by the time I complete the process.

The blade slips a few times when I'm separating the skin, but it's mostly in one piece when I begin to peel it back, exposing a grizzly mask of red flesh and golden fat. I'm really pleased with how this came out. It's a miracle I didn't sever her jugular or carotid while I was working. I stand back to admire my work.

The skin from her face and neck is now bunched up on her chest. Her pale eyelids still blink from the mess of her face. Her nose, thicker with cartilage, is also untouched. I left her lips, too. The skin there was too thin for me to take the extra time to remove. Everything is smeared with her own blood.

She starts retching, leaning to the side, trying not to vomit on herself. There's nowhere for her to go. I wait 'til she gets sick down her chest. Miraculously, only a few bits get stuck in her wounds.

I think she might be right, though. Something else is killing her. Something other than me. And I don't think it's the ill-placed vibrator.

"Could you turn on the fan?" she pleads. "Get some air in here? I'm lightheaded, dizzy. I think it's too hot."

"Well," I say, feeling a little disappointed, "you're not going to be much fun anymore. Do you have a heart condition? If so, you really should have told a doctor. If I had seen that in my research, I would've handled this differently."

She's looking at the TV now, with a sort of delirious glassiness in her eyes. The video is still playing, a sort of highlights of her years with him. She seems mesmerized.

Part of me wants to turn it off, not let her have this while she's dying, but I need investigators to know what she's done. And there's a kind of poetry to him being just out of her reach. I retrieve the captive bolt from my backpack and step between her and the screen, so I'm the one filling up her vision.

Even if I did like guns, I wouldn't use hers.

"Please," she begs, "just let me look at him."

"No," I say, putting the bolt against her head. "I'm going to put you down just like the animal you are."

I pull the trigger.

ABBY

THIRTY-FIVE

The captive bolt is messier than I thought it would be. It's obvious after the fact, a shock of air pushing a metal shaft into the head at a high rate of speed seems likely to cause a splash, but at least the bone fragments stay inside the head. It doesn't do much for the bleeding, though. Head wounds bleed a lot. Well, she's not bleeding because dead bodies don't do that, but there is a lot of splatter. And despite my painter's suit, there's still some brain matter on me. That's not ideal.

I try to be pragmatic about it, but it still makes me nauseous. There are a few rules of murder. One is, don't leave DNA at the scene, which means no vomit. Sweat may be negligible, but a pile of barf would draw more attention. I gag and swallow hard, trying my best to keep it down. Once it comes up, there isn't much you can do about it, and I don't want to give investigators more to work with, even if they don't have anything to match it against.

I step into the trash bag I opened before I started working and unzip the suit, letting it puddle around me on the floor. I take the latex off, hooking my index and middle finger of my right hand under the edge of the glove on the left so I don't get any blood or brain matter on my skin. I change my shoe covers too.

The TV plays behind me, and I do my best to tune it out. My job is weird, but everything has gotten very morbid. Having sex sounds in the background with a dead body on the bed when that dead body was one of the people making sex sounds is disturbing.

Gloria was a terrible person. If she hadn't died—if I hadn't killed her—she would have had Matt murdered, then she would have done this to another boy.

That's the truth.

And I'm the one who stopped her.

I bundle up my things, but leave the cut rope segments behind.

I slip her cellphone out of my pocket and lay it back on the nightstand where I snatched it from. I take off the mesh metal gloves and put them into the backpack, then I put on a fresh pair of gloves over the pair I already had on. I roll the trash bag up carefully, double-bag it, I stuff it into my backpack.

I leave the bolt lying on the bed next to Gloria's corpse.

Before I leave the house, there's a few more things I need to do. I have to take the cameras down. I expect that will be much faster than putting them in.

And with Matt tied in the torture room, now is the only time I'll be able to do this.

But I do hate the idea of leaving him there all night. From what I've seen, the housekeeper doesn't get in 'til at least 8 or 9 in the morning. And since it's only just now after midnight, that means he'll have a minimum of seven hours before someone gets to the house.

It could be a lot longer before someone notices something is wrong. How long it takes the housekeeper to work through the house and where she starts is variable.

I know I have the time to finish going through the house. Once I'm done looking through the safe, I can evaluate how much longer he may have to wait.

After I take the equipment down, I go to check on something. The videos she was watching sparked a memory in me.

There are aspects of this case that feel familiar. Things that are too close to be a coincidence.

We're awfully close to the town Percilla mentioned for this not to be somehow related. There's the money, the location, and people who happen to have abuse as a hobby. Some circles are just too small to be accidental, and I wouldn't be surprised if Gloria was a part of a circle that used to own me and maybe my mother, too.

THIRTY-SIX

Gloria's office is tidy and elegant. The safe is in the obvious point of command behind the centered desk, hidden behind a piece of art that looked like a Picasso print. Fitting, given everything else about this situation. Of course, she has the work of another abuser hanging on her wall. I pull on the corner, just as I saw Gloria open it. The frame releases from a latch that holds it shut.

I turn the dial on the safe, back and forth until the hollow click sounds. I twist the handle. The door swings open.

There's a small brown leather notebook at the top of the stack. It says passwords across the top. I open it and flip through. Inside, there is a list of sites, logins, and passwords.

The password for her computer is at the front.

Her email is already pulled up when I log in, too. I look back at her recently sent messages.

There's one with a name I recognize. Roland Jackson. He was in the article Percilla sent me.

But how does Gloria know him? I search her email and see there's a history of them going back a long time.

There's an email about Matt. Except in the email, his name is Matteo, and he is six years old. He has a family. There's an email to my father with a note where he says he'll keep more of Gloria's papers.

Her last email says that it's time for a new one.

I got here just in time.

There's a faint tapping sound.

I freeze, then listen, straining my ears.

The house is silent again.

I tuck the notebook in my pocket, then take out the stack of papers under it.

There's a folder for each of the women from the brunch, labeled with their names and a headshot clipped to the cover. Inside is a bio, with likes and dislikes and a list of attributes. It almost looks like a dating service. Then I see the information listed for the potential matches for each of them. Young boys. Adoptions, maybe.

Then I see a folder with Gloria's name on it.

There's an old picture of a boy. He looks a lot like Matt. There are several other boys in the folder, but they all have a red stamp, *disqualified*, on the top. But the boy who looks like Matt says, approved.

I shove the papers from the safe into my bag and turn to the door. I need to get out of the house, but it feels weird leaving this stuff behind. These are people I could save.

Matt is standing in the doorway, the revolver in his shaking right hand, and he's looking at me with shifting eyes. "If you just give me the papers, I'll go. I won't say anything about what's happened here."

I swallow hard, my mouth feeling like it's been filled with sand.

He's wearing dark sweatpants, a matching sweatshirt, and has a gym duffle hanging down his back. "Look, I'm just trying to get away," he says, his voice pleading. "I just need my passport, and I can go."

Stepping back away from him, I fumble inside my bag, pulling out the sheaf of papers. I keep an eye on him as I search for the folder with his name on it. When I find it, I place it on the desk and step away. "There. It's all yours."

He doesn't hesitate to step forward and start digging through the packet. "It's not here."

There's a look of panic in his eyes.

I search my bag again. Neither of us should be in this room, and he should never have come back into the house. "That's all I found about you."

Headlights flash through the front window, and we both turn to see who is there. A lifted truck with dark tinted windows rolls to a stop, its brights trained on the front of the house.

"We have to go now." I say, starting past him, heading for the door. I need to get him out of here. After all the work I've done to keep him safe, to give him an alibi. How has he walked right back into this mess? Now he won't have a solid defense for the investigators. They'll never believe he wasn't involved.

"You don't understand," he says. "Without it, I have nothing. I wasn't born here. If I don't have my paperwork, they'll deport me. They'll take everything from me if I can't prove my citizenship."

Turning back to the window, I peek into the night. No one has gotten out yet.

"Okay, fine," I say, already second-guessing my decision. "Come keep an eye on the truck. Tell me if anyone gets out."

I wake the computer. It prompts for the password again. I grab the notebook from my bag and flip to the first page. After I type in the password and hit enter, the welcome screen spins. Gloria's name pops up, and I'm back to her email. I type in the email search bar looking for my father's name again, this time looking for his contact card. Roland's home address isn't far from here, and I'm pretty sure that is where Matt's passport is.

I know it's a terrible idea, but I've been looking for him. This confrontation was bound to happen, even if this isn't how I thought it would go.

Peeling a sticky note off the stack on the desk, I write the address down then look it up on a map so I know where we're going. When I'm done, I put the note in my pocket. "Okay, time to go. Is there a back way out?" I ask to put him at ease. I don't want him to know I've seen every square inch of this place.

That I've been watching for days.

My van is at least a mile away. There is no way I can make it there without having to walk past the truck. It's parked near the large barn with a clear line of sight across the fields and down the driveway.

Not ideal.

"Someone's coming," Matt says, tearing his gaze from the window then darting a look back out into the night.

"We need to get out the back, and we need to go now." I grab his wrist, making him flinch.

The burns.

"I'm so sorry," I say, letting go.

"Yeah," he mutters, but he follows me.

The sprawling ranch style has large fixed windows all around, but it's pitch black outside, aside from the ultra bright lights from the truck. But if we can get out the side and away from the high beams, by the time their eyes adjust, we'll be long gone.

It would be nicer to leave through a door, but I think the best way out is from a low casement that opens to the side over the garden from the sunroom. There's a long hall with windows facing the front of the house, and we have to get down on our bellies and crawl to be sure no one can see us. The glow of the lights is faint. When I get to the door, I reach up and turn the knob. The door swings open with a groan.

The doorbell chimes, and then I hear Gloria's phone ringing from her bedroom just up the hall from us.

He looks frightened, still shaking. He has the gun that was in the nightstand in one hand, and the folder in the other. I know he saw what I did to her, even though I left the door closed.

The doorbell rings again, and I start moving across the sunroom to one of the windows that opens out. There's a shadow. A man, walking through the garden.

I duck my head and look back over my shoulder. The door to the room is open behind us, and Matt is standing there still as a statue.

The shadow moves past.

Matt ducks down next to me.

Gloria's phone starts to ring again.

I reach for the window latch to unlock it and I see another figure move past us outside. They're circling the house, and I'm not sure how many of them there are, but we have to get out and make one of the outbuildings or the tree line before they come inside.

Someone starts hammering on one of the front windows, the glass pane rattling in its frame.

They're getting closer.

"What do we do?" Matt whispers.

Holding my breath, I lift the latch. The clicking sound it makes feels a million times louder, if only because our silence is imperative. I open it a little at a time, pausing to listen for footsteps.

It's quiet.

I sit on the windowsill and pull off the shoe covers I've been wearing, then climb out, mulch crunching under my feet as I step down. I wave my hand for Matt to follow me.

He swings his legs over, then lurches, nearly falling when a door crashes open behind him.

"Aw shit! Roland, we've got a problem!" a man shouts.

I grab the scruff of Matt's shirt and haul him down below the ledge. We're both breathing heavily, but the thud of boots running away in the house is enough to give us cover. We keep moving toward the big barn, staying near the shrubs at the side of the house.

I glance over my shoulder toward the truck. All the doors are open, and the lights inside the house have started to come on.

Matt still has his folder clutched to his chest.

Did I close the safe? I can't remember, and it's too late to do anything about it now. I stop behind the large oak tree in the front yard and look back toward the house. I can see five figures moving inside.

One comes back out the front and retches into the grass by the walkway. He wipes his mouth with his sleeve, then walks to the back of the truck.

We wait 'til he goes inside the vehicle, then we start toward the fence that lines the first pasture. We follow it to the first barn.

"How quickly can you saddle a horse?" I ask Matt.

"Pretty fast," he says.

I nod. "Okay," I add as an afterthought, realizing the gesture was probably lost in the dark. "You get the horses, and I'll get the tack?"

In the tack room, I grab two bridles off the wall and loop them over my arm, then I grab two saddles and saddle clothes that are on the rack closest to the door.

The first horse is already tied outside, the lead rope fastened with a quick-release clove hitch.

I put the tack on some wooden crates to free up my hands, then take the saddle blanket I'm going to use.

"Hey, I'm just going to put this saddle on you," I whisper, keeping up a steady stream of talk so the horse doesn't spook.

First, I run my hands over the horse's back, checking for burrs or anything that might cause discomfort when the rest of the tack is in place. Second, I line up the saddle pad. After that, I swing the saddle over the top of it and make sure everything is lined up again.

Matt is back, leading one of the other horses.

"Where's the gun?" I whisper, noticing that he's not holding it or the folder in his hands.

He ties the horse next to me and starts to saddle it. "I put them in the bag. Should I leave it here?"

I cinch the girth strap, then slip my fingers between the fabric and the animal, making sure it's tight enough. I pull the bridle over the halter and lead rope. "Leave the gun. It will be hard to get rid of."

He nods, pausing to stash it in the barrel of sweet feed. He still finishes saddling his horse first. It's no surprise that Matt is much faster than I am.

We mount quickly and start off without a word.

The gates between the pastures are already open, so it's no problem to ride from Gloria's house to the neighboring property.

This is my father's address listed in Gloria's email.

The horses are familiar with the grounds, which only further confirms my suspicion. And they don't seem to mind the night ride, which is a good thing because I can't afford one more hiccup.

The fence leads up to a small overgrown garden with a fountain in it, but the whole area is hidden from the drive.

The windows above are dark, and I'm confident I can get into the house without being seen, especially since the driveway is empty.

"Look, this will be a lot easier and a lot faster if you wait outside."

He nods.

I go into my father's house alone.

THIRTY-SEVEN

The front door isn't locked. It isn't even latched.

I don't know my way around this place, so I have no choice but to go through each floor, room by room.

The house is old.

This kind of property costs more money to keep up than is usually worth it to the casual home buyer, but this place belongs to an old family. The creaking floorboards threaten to give me away, which is inconvenient.

I'm starting to realize how incredibly stupid it was to come in here on the word of one of the victims I'm trying to save. How do I know for sure he doesn't have his passport? It's not likely that he's working with them, but it's not completely impossible.

If I make it out of this alive, Percilla is going to kill me. Leave the shelter of Mother Mercy, come down here to Virginia, and string me up by my pinky toes.

The chandelier in the entry hall is lit with a faint glow where the lights have been turned down, but not off. French doors covered in white curtains lead off of the entry hall into various rooms that I have yet to explore. A wide staircase wraps around the room, against the right side of the hall and behind me over my head.

I take the first door on the left, where there's a little light.

The room is empty. The ambient glow from outside—where the garden light is illuminating the wild roses and tall elegant windows—filters in. It seems to be a breakfast room with wood lattice floors that echo when I step, even muffled a bit by the shoe covers. The kitchen is through the door at the back of the room. It is badly in need of modernization. Next to it are several storage closets. I head back to the main hall.

I spot a doorway under the stairs. Based on the marble threshold, I know it's a hall bathroom so I skip it and go through the set of French doors under the stairs.

Office space and a dead end.

I go back out to the entryway below the grand staircase. There are two more sets of French doors, one to the right and one to the left, with three more sets leading out the back of the house.

This time, I go to the right.

It's a library filled with old books, some are in lit cases, thick spines opened for display.

Across the hall, the French doors stand open to what seems like a sitting room with a grand piano. The outer wall is made up of French doors as well, all windows and sheer curtains with low couches grouped in the center of the room. I take out my flashlight, keeping it on the dimmest setting, and examine the pictures on the end tables. The faces are not just familiar. I *know* some of them.

I recognize my mom and one of the men pictured in the news clipping about her death. I can only assume it's Roland since this was his address saved in Gloria's computer.

I stop, fumbling to turn up the brightness on my flashlight.

Why is Percilla in some of these photos?

I turn from one frame to another. She's in a lot of the pictures, standing next to a big man with broad shoulders, a square jaw, and short dark hair. He's tanned as if he spends a lot of time outside. In one photo, he has an arm draped over her shoulder possessively. He holds a brown beer bottle up toward the camera, and her head is nearly tucked under his armpit like a football.

He's grinning broadly, but Percilla is stone-faced. She doesn't even try to look at the camera. Her gaze cast down, looking at the ground. I open the frame and look at the back. It says the photo is of Mark and Beth Ballanger.

There's another photo labeled, "the Jackson boys:" Richard, William, and Thomas. But I'm not sure if it has their names in order.

I spot an old picture that looks like it's from Judge and Mrs. Jackson's wedding.

Gloria is there in another photo, too, standing next to a young boy I don't recognize and the Jackson sons. It looks like it was taken at a wedding. There are no names on that one, but if she's related by marriage, that would explain a lot.

Finally, in the center of the table, there's a small framed photo. *That's my family.* Me, Mom, and the man who killed her.

I put the backs on the frames and try not to leave things looking as messy as I've made them, though I can't remember where everything was when I first came in.

There's a ringing in my ears as I step back. I'm in shock. Logic seems just out of my reach.

I can't let this distract me. There's too much at stake, and I'm on unfamiliar ground.

I turn to leave.

When I open my eyes, my head aches and I can't tell where I am. It takes a moment for the haze to clear and for me to realize there is black fabric over my head. Outside the bag, I can make out a bright light in the room, but that's about it.

I have a sinking feeling in the pit of my stomach when I realize I've fucked up. I was too focused on everything except what really mattered, and now I'm royally screwed.

Actually, I might already be dead.

Someone snatches the bag off my head. Blinding bright light flashes into my eyes. I blink hard to regain my sight. A shaggy-haired, gum-chewing man grins at me.

"Hey, sweetheart," he says, blowing a bubble and sucking it back between his lips 'til it pops.

I scowl.

"Boy, your daddy's gonna be happy to see you," he grins, taking out a phone and punching in some numbers.

Keeping an eye on him, I discreetly glance around, trying to get my bearings. He looks like the man from the beach in South Carolina.

I'm sure he's killed someone before, so I have to be careful.

From the little bit of the space I can see, we're in the same house, but not in one of the rooms I explored. I'm a little confused as to whom he is talking, but I think he is talking to Roland. They were calling his name when they barged into Gloria's house, but it's still not clear who everyone is or how they're related. Are they my uncles? Did they know my mother? Did they have kids?

I know my father killed my mother. I just need to hear him say it to my face.

"Hey, boss," he says, talking louder than necessary, "I've got your daughter. Clocked her pretty good, but she's handcuffed in your office. No additional damage." He chuckles. "Sure, just waitin' on you!"

He hangs up the phone and takes a seat across from me in a straight-backed wooden chair, resting his elbow on the desk beside him.

My backpack is next to him. It doesn't look like he's gone through it…yet. It's still zipped all the way shut, and it's not bulging like it would be if anyone had tried to repack it.

"We're just waiting?" I ask, not really caring about his answer.

He's sitting in front of me, and my hands are cuffed behind my back, which is the best-case scenario. I shift my foot around as I test the cuffs he put me in, seeing how much I can move without making a lot of noise.

He raises a brow and blows another bubble. "What, you want to talk now? I thought you just wanted to break in and sneak around."

"I don't know. Perhaps you can help me find what I'm looking for," I shrug. "Maybe not, though. It doesn't really seem like you're the brains." I'm not as worried now that I know Roland wants to talk to me and doesn't seem to want me dead. I already would be if that were the plan. So, I just need to work the key that's up my sleeve down a bit so I can get out of these silver bracelets and make a break for it.

"Oh," he laughs. "You're so feisty."

"It's fine if you're too scared to think for yourself," I quip even though I know he's not going to take the bait. I'm just trying to cover the sound. I roll the band down my arm further, working the key toward my palm. There is another positive about them having some kind of plan for me. They haven't called the cops. I'm not sure why they made such a bold move, but I'm not going to question the one good thing that's happened since Matt found me in Gloria's office.

"And if I could think for myself, what would I be thinking?" he leans forward, really looking at me now.

That's not exactly what I wanted, but okay. "Who's the big meathead in the pictures?"

"Oh," he says, making a ridiculous sad face in mock hurt. "Straight for the good stuff."

"If you don't know, that's okay." I shrug like I don't care, but it's really just enough movement for me to get the key from my right wrist into my palm and shift it between my fingers. Now I just need him distracted enough that I can work it into the lock without rattling the chains too loudly.

"You can't seriously expect me to tell you," he says with a laugh.

I don't answer. I have no reason to believe that he has the full picture. There's no way he's met Percilla and knows that she's familiar with me.

He might suspect Roland is my father, but maybe I'm just a girl that his boss is after.

Based on Roland's emails to Gloria, I'm almost certain they're in the business of trafficking people. But there's no way for me to interrogate him for useful information without giving away that I already know more than I should.

He might not even know about Roland's wife, my mother.

Would my father ever admit that his wife ran from him? That he couldn't keep her, that she tried to leave him, and that—rather than face that truth—he killed her?

"You good?" He asks, leaning forward.

"What?" He must have said something I didn't respond to.

"I might have hit you harder than I thought."

"You didn't hit me that hard," I say with a smile.

"Yeah, you were out cold for a while, because I didn't hit you that hard. Right…"

"No, yeah, totally." He's cocky. I can use that. "I was just wondering if they ever figured out who murdered Roland's wife?"

"Who?"

"Your boss, Roland. He had a wife." I decide to needle him by adding, "But I guess you didn't know that."

He looks uncertain now. The bubble blowing stops, and he eyes me warily. "Now you're just fuckin' with me, huh," he says, although it sounds a bit like a question. When he laughs, it sounds forced.

He thought someone in his position would be safe, that he could be close enough to the boss that he wouldn't have to worry about the kinds of things organizations like this do to other people.

The kinds of things I do to other people, too.

It hadn't occurred to him that his value isn't as high as he thought it was. That there are things he's been left out of that might change the decisions he would have made.

Regardless, sometimes accountability feels like retribution. And that is something I intend to teach him very soon.

He starts chewing again, still thinking.

"It's true," I say in my best nonchalant tone.

He leans forward again, the weight of his gaze doing its best to drill into me.

I do everything in one smooth movement.

I shift the circle of the handcuffs onto my fist like the grip of brass knuckles. I lean forward, dropping my weight to the side and sling my arm and shoulder forward in an arching motion 'til my fist connects with his windpipe.

Surprise flashes on his face, his hands clutch his throat, a half-blown bubble sags on his lips. He slides out of his chair and falls face-first, hitting the floor with a heavy thud.

Piercing bright lights flash behind me as the truck from next door pulls into the driveway.

THIRTY-EIGHT

I go to the body on the floor, checking his pockets for weapons. I take the gun from the back of his pants and transfer it to mine, then I flip him over. I don't have long to be pleased about how hard I hit him, but he won't be getting up anytime soon. With CPR, there's a chance he might make it, but without medical attention, a broken hyoid is lethal.

I have no intention of taking the gun with me, but I'm not going to leave it where it can be used against me. And while I can shoot, in my line of work, it's not the best way to take out the trash.

I could find somewhere to hide in this house, but as much as it goes against my survival instincts, I did come here to see Roland. It's a greater risk for me. I know I never should have come here, but *should* isn't going to fix anything. And this is my chance to learn the truth.

A quick glance out the window of Roland's office tells me I'm on the second floor. A quick escape through the window? Not an option. Not to mention the vaulted ceilings below make this feel more like the third. I can't see much else other than the lights.

I check the desk, looking for more weapons. Under the chairs, too. I know he's coming, so I have to be quick, tugging at picture frames, and anything large enough to look like it might be a hiding place for a weapon. He might not want to end my life, but I'm not going to risk him having a weapon that will make it easier for him to hurt me.

In the end, I find some extra handcuffs in the desk, a few spare keys, and another gun. I retrieve my backpack and put the items in it for now, just so he doesn't have access to them. When I hear footsteps on the stairs, I move away from the door, perching on one of the wide windowsills by the tall front windows that overlook the circular drive.

He looks different from what I remember. Older. To be fair, it has been over twenty years.

Momma told him I was at school the day he killed her.

He has no way of knowing that I listened to it happen from my hiding place under the winter coats in the closet by the front door.

"Mara," he says, stepping into the room and closing the door behind him.

I nod in greeting, but I don't say anything.

Jesse must have taken photos of me on the beach. That, and a quick de-aging process, are the only explanation for why he can recognize me on sight.

He glances around the room, eyeing the dead man on the floor. "I'm impressed. Jessie was one of the good ones."

"I'd hate to see what one of the bad ones look like. He didn't seem to know much about what was going on here. He didn't know about my mother."

"Well, your *mother* had it coming. It's obvious she always intended to keep you from me. I'm not surprised you think the worst."

"It's hard not to, since you killed her. Wouldn't it be more surprising if I were fine with that?"

"You were a child. I don't think there's any way you could understand. It was an adult situation."

"I think I understand pretty well. I was there."

He looks surprised at that. "Where?"

"In the closet. I was there the whole time while you beat my mother. When you shot her."

I can see he's trying to justify what he did in his mind, using the new information to make up a new story that suits his narrative.

"So is that it?" I ask, feigning boredom with the conversation. "Do I have any family worth knowing?"

"Is that why you came back? To see if there was anyone *other* than me?" Anger and bitterness bleed into his tone.

"I certainly didn't come back to forgive you," I scoff. "There's nothing you could do to earn it from me."

"I don't need to earn anything from you. I don't care what you think about what I've done. That woman deserved it. You don't know what she was like."

"Then why didn't you leave? If she was so awful? Why didn't *you* run? It seems like you have plenty of money."

"Is that what you want from me? Money?" he scoffs. "I swear, women are all the same."

My laugh is harsh and bitter. "I don't need anything from you. I'd *like* to have answers. I want to know if I have any other family, but I'm fine never knowing." Or, I will be now that I've met my father again. "I always land on my feet, and I've been standing on my own from the moment you walked out of my life." I don't tell him that I have support, that there is someone in the world who will always love me, even when I'm selfish, ungrateful, and make stupid mistakes. Like coming here. I don't tell him about the dog I had growing up with Percilla, or that I've never been alone and I never will be. I don't tell him about the papers I'm looking for either. That will guarantee he won't give them to me.

"How much do you want?" he asks, opening the wall safe. "I have plenty of cash."

"I don't want your blood money," I answer as he opens the safe. I wish I could stuff the words back in as soon as they're out. The documents I need are in there. This is the only way Matt can disappear and have any hope of a normal life.

"No, really, how much?"

He takes out stacks of papers and places them on the desk.

"How about one hundred thousand?" I ask, egging him on.

He glances at me, burning rage simmering on his face. He's so angry, he's trembling. I know I've pushed him to the brink.

I remember this clearly. The tipping point where he loses his mind and forgets all the apologies from the times before.

When he turns back to the safe to get the money, I stand and make my way over to the desk, keeping it between us.

He places six stacks of bills bound with mustard-colored bands on the desk, then turns around to get the other four.

I lunge for the papers.

He spins around, grabs my wrist, and snatches them from my grasping fingers.

I don't know why I didn't try to kill him.

If it were anyone else, it would have been the first thing I did.

He drags me over the top of it by my arm. The hardware on my backpack scrapes across the smooth finish of leather and wood. Both the money and manila folders fall and skitter across the floor.

His right hand comes down like a vice on my throat.

The tools in my bag dig into my spine. My boot heels scrabble off the end of the desk, flailing in the air.

He has my right arm pinned beside me, so I reach around with my left hand and grab his thumb, trying to loosen his grasp.

Unhelpful facts filter through my panic.

Men who choke women end up killing them. Maybe not the first time, but always eventually.

Most hyoid fractures are caused by hanging or strangulation.

It can take as little as five to ten seconds to lose consciousness. A few more minutes for death to occur.

He doesn't speak. His rage is all-consuming, like the lights are on, but no one is home.

Spots swim in the corners of my eyes. I don't have much time. I reach into my pocket and grab the small folding knife I keep there for everyday use. I flip it open with my thumb and stab it into his arm. I'm aiming for his bicep, but I get closer to the ditch of his elbow.

He lets me go, unable to maintain his grasp with the knife where it is.

The expression on his face is confusion, more than rage now.

I push away from him, falling off the desk as I do so, and leave the knife behind as I crawl away, gasping for air.

This isn't going well.

The papers are scattered out and their folders open like books. There are pictures, more faces, not quite mugshots, but the people in those pictures don't look happy or safe. It's even more important than before that I survive.

Not just for Percilla and Matt, but for all the other people they have stolen. I can save them if I make it out alive.

Leaning heavily on the edge of a chair, I finally stand up.

Roland is stalking toward me, holding the knife he pulled from his arm. It looks like a toothpick clutched in his fist.

He's a big man, and his anger seems to fill up the room, vaulted ceiling and all.

My impulse is to retreat, then I remember the gun at my back. I reach for it, whip it out. But I should have thought about the safety first. It's on, and it's stuck.

I haven't practiced with guns in a long time. I don't use them because they're too traceable, and right now that fact is coming back to bite me in the ass.

I switch the safety off.

His hand engulfs mine and, as he strips the gun away, it goes off, firing a shot into the door. He barrels me backward into the wall, scraping me across it like a rag doll he's using to polish the wainscoting.

The gun skids away, under one of the sofas on the other side of the room.

With my hands free, I use both of them to grasp his thumbs and yank them back and down toward the floor, forcing his grip to release. With the wall at my back, I don't try to pull away. I push forward, crowding him, and bring my knee up between his legs as hard as I can.

He groans and sags to one knee, catching himself with a fist against the floor and grasping at his crotch.

I grab the back of his head, forcing it forward as I bring my knee up to meet his face.

He takes the brunt of the blow with his forehead, wrapping his arms around me as he rolls me onto the floor.

This is very not good.

He laughs. "You put up more of a fight than your mother."

I lunge for him, raking my nails across his face, leaving pink tracks that begin to ooze red blood.

When he swings for me, I duck my head to the side, his fist crashing into the floor beside my ear with a thud.

Before he can pull back, I sink my teeth into his hand and rip a chunk of flesh away. I scratch all along his arms, and he grasps my throat again, but rage fuels me. Rage and hate and fear.

The taste of blood fills my mouth, and I fight the urge to spit it in his face.

He draws back.

I plant my feet flat on the floor and buck up, throwing him off balance, then twist away from him. I grab the legs of a nearby chair and spin around, cracking it into his outstretched arms.

I crawl toward the gun on the floor where he flung it away, feeling with my hand in the dark gap under the couch.

The office door flies open, crashing into the wall with a bang.

Matt has a brass fire poker in his hands. He crosses the room in a few strides and swings at Roland, the flat side striking his arm.

Roland grabs the hook, yanking it toward him.

Matt doesn't let go.

"You've got yourself a little boy toy!" My father guffaws. "How does old Gloria feel about that?"

He chuckles at his own joke.

Matt doesn't join in. "Gloria isn't feeling much these days," he says, keeping his eyes on my father.

Roland is fast, wrenching the poker from Matt's grasp and pulling him into a headlock. He pulls the bar of the poker up against his neck trying to choke him.

Matt grips the metal and drops like a stone, throwing Roland off balance. My father tips forward as Matt rolls away from him and to the side.

My fingers brush the rough grip on the butt of the gun.

Roland comes up, standing over Matt with the poker poised to strike a deadly blow.

I roll onto my back and aim the gun at my father's chest.

I pull the trigger.

THIRTY-NINE

Whistling breath echo from my father as we shift the furniture to make sure no documents are left behind.

We don't talk as we gather the rest of the papers from the floor and dominating desk.

I'm not sure where my DNA might have ended up. Botched crime scene cleanup is one of the things that get a lot of people caught. This time, I have to try harder. There's traceable parts of me here and half of the solution to the puzzle is laying dead on the rug.

If they run my DNA against his, they're going to get more than they bargained for, and I'm going to be in deep shit.

It's a little late, but I offer shoe covers to Matt and pull new ones on where the others were stripped from my boots. I open a trash bag and put my old ones in.

My father is still twitching on the floor, but I take tissues from the box that was knocked from the desk and wipe his face clean and the spot where I bit him.

I get peroxide from the first-aid kit in my bag and pour it over the wound, trying to remove my saliva.

Then I wipe the face and arms of the dead guy, clean the grip on the gun, and put it in his hand since it was his, anyway.

My father's dazed eyes follow me, but he can hardly move.

When I shot him from the floor, I'm pretty sure the upward angle of the bullet punctured his lung and severed his spinal cord.

When I bend over him, his glassy gaze shifts, trying to focus on me.

"You did come looking for me, didn't you?" I ask. "You tracked, what's her name, Beth? And you figured out what she was up to? But you couldn't have us out here, picking off your customers. I think Gloria might have been the first one, but I'm sure we'll find more. Now that your Grandaddy's dead, who's going to bury all the family secrets? Like your boy Jessie, who saw me at the beach?"

I pull his shirt up until I can wad enough fabric in my hands and hold it down over his mouth and nose.

"Doesn't really matter, does it?"

I look into his eyes. As I do, they shift around wildly, filled with terror. His arms aren't moving. I don't think they physically can.

"I don't know," I say, so only he can hear me. "I think my mom put up more of a fight than you did."

My grin is forced and maybe a little bloody, but I want it to be the last thing he sees. I keep my gaze locked on his, even as his sight blurs. I keep my hands over his face, feeling the strain in his movements as he fights for breath. I keep the pressure there 'til he stops moving and I'm sure he's dead.

Even when his muscles stop twitching, I stay where I am, just to be extra sure.

I take a deep breath, counting to four, to steady my nerves. I hold for four, then exhale for four again. I take my hands away slowly, watching him carefully even though he's dead.

The rest of the cleanup is methodical. I put the trash in the garbage bag I'm carrying, then take the papers from Matt and shove it all into my overstuffed backpack.

Lastly, I retrieve my knife. "We need to go," I say and start toward the door. I don't wait to see if he follows me, but I hear his footsteps on the hardwood behind me. I pick up the pace.

The horses are by the fence outside where we left them. I pull myself up and swing into the saddle. Matt does the same beside me. More bright lights break across the tree line behind us as someone turns down the long winding drive. We spur our horses into motion and turn them back toward the front pasture of Gloria's house.

Matt doesn't ask any questions. He just follows me.

I'm so far out of my depth. I've never brought anyone in, and I don't know what to do. But I'm taking him to the van because I don't think either of us has any other options. I'm guessing they aren't the only ones working for my father. I don't know if my uncles are involved, but someone is going to be looking for people who shouldn't be in the area. If Matt gets picked up, would they kill him? I have no way of knowing, but I know they would be one step closer to me, and I can't have that.

I don't even want to call Percilla because then I would be putting her safety at risk. Especially with her picture here, with a husband that knew these people. I don't know if he's still alive.

Now I know why she asked me to stay away.

Look what I've done.

When we get to the front of the pasture, we walk to the tree line and remove the tack, leaving their bridles, saddles, and saddle blankets in the stand of trees so they won't tangle in the horses' legs and injure them. They don't deserve that.

We watch the road to make sure no cars are coming, then we climb the fence and run across the street.

The van is where I left it.

I fish my keys out of the front pocket on the backpack, then unlock the door and climb in.

Matt stands there, looking at me with a hand in his pocket. With his other, he holds the duffel bag on his shoulder, not sure what to do.

"We have to go," I urge him.

"Where?" he seems confused, dazed a little.

"Out of state, for starters."

"We just killed that guy."

"That's why we have to go," I say, irritation washing over me.

"Are you going to kill me?" he asks, looking more tired than anything else.

"What?" A shocked laugh bubbles out of me. "No! You think I went through all of that just to kill you?"

"You came here for me?" he asks as he walks around the front of the van and climbs into the passenger seat.

"I got a message saying you were in trouble." I'm intentionally vague about how I got the letter.

"That's crazy," he muses. "I just didn't think anyone would listen or care."

He's quiet for a while before asking, "Do you know who it was?"

"It said it was from a parent," I say.

He eyes me warily. "That can't be right. My parents are dead."

I hesitate before I ask, but I have to know. "Do you have any kids?"

He shakes his head.

"Thank goodness for that."

My stomach does a little flip-flop. One less thing I'll have to worry about later. I'm starting to think that Roland wasn't so much looking for me as he was Percilla. I'll have the chance to ask her more questions now that I can assure her my father won't be coming after either of us again. But I don't know how much anyone else in his employ might know, and you don't smuggle people across the border without some kind of organization.

I head toward I81. We can take it all the way to upstate New York if we have to, but I figure we'll be in the clear well before then.

After about an hour of driving, we stop behind a church and put a new wrap on the van. Black, this time. Then it's back on the road.

Matt falls asleep.

I watch the sun come up as we cross the state line into Maryland, but I don't stop 'til we cross into Pennsylvania. There's a rest area there. I park in a corner close to the tree line and pull the shades over the windows. I let Matt sleep while I change into clean clothes and stuff the others into my laundry bag. I still need to get rid of the trash bag from the house, but I'm not going to leave it here.

I take the keys and a new burner phone when I get out of the van and make the call.

After five rings, she answers.

"I'm okay," I say, before she has the chance to ask. "But something has happened."

Her breath hitches when I get to the part about the pictures, when I tell her the names I saw and the faces I recognized.

EPILOGUE

I've never been to Connecticut before, but it's beautiful here. This small town is well off my beaten path. Matt has been here once before, with Gloria, though he doesn't talk about it.

I don't ask him to.

When I asked him where he wanted to go, this was the place he chose. And even though I'm curious, I don't pry.

At first, it was strange having him climb into the queen bed in the back of my van with me. Strange for him, too, I guess.

When I asked Matt how he got out of the tack room, I also told him I had left him there so none of the blame would fall on him, and how I'll still make sure he's in the clear.

That's when he told me it wasn't the first time Gloria had left him tied up like that. One time, it had been for three days. After, he decided to hide a key in a small notch he'd carved out of the sawhorse. He'd then covered it with wood putty so she wouldn't find it.

Smart.

We've been on the road for days and, though he's offered to drive, I haven't felt comfortable with that. Now that we've stopped running, there's nothing to occupy the silence between us.

He doesn't want to talk anymore about what I may have seen, and I don't know how to tell him about how I really got there.

I have a strong suspicion Roland sent Percilla the note himself.

I'm glad my father is dead. I'm relieved he'll never be able to hunt Percilla down. And I believe, after this, the two of us will be a lot better at talking about our pasts. I think we're both sorry we didn't listen to each other. But I'm glad we have answers now.

It's strange to realize that I've killed both my father and my aunt, even if she wasn't related to me by blood. For him, I know that's patricide. For her, is it familicide? Because she married into the family?

Percilla tells me not to dwell on it too much. And while I try not to, I can't help but think about it sometimes.

"We're in a tough situation," she says.

I can hear the worry in her tone, and I know that she's trying to sort out the consequences of my actions.

"I'm sorry," I say.

Percilla sighs. "It's already done. All we can do is figure out what to do next."

"I know I fucked this up." I say. The 'I should have listened to you' goes unsaid, but so does the accusation that she should have trusted me. "Was Mark friends with Roland?"

"They were cousins," she says.

I'm so surprised that she answered me without a fight, that my mouth hangs open for a second.

Somehow, even though she can't see me, she knows.

"Close your mouth," she says, "or you'll catch flies."

We laugh, and a sense of relief washes over me, knowing she's not going to bring up those things either. We can get past this. We'll be okay. "I want to come home."

"I know," she says, sounding wistful.

But there's nothing either of us can do until we figure out this thing with Matt. We still don't know how he feels about everything we do or what he wants.

"I love you," I say.

She says it back, and I hang up the phone.

Matt is quiet. He has been for the past few weeks while we've moved from one campground to another. I guess we both have been.

I finally think I know what I want to say. When I roll onto my side, ready to speak, he's looking up at the ceiling and there are tears running down his face.

He doesn't move, so I turn onto my back and look up at the roof of the van, too.

I shift my hand 'til the back of my fingers graze against his.

He doesn't pull away, so I take his hand in mine and let our fingers twist together.

It's comforting, not being alone on the road anymore. And for better or worse, it looks like, at least for the time being, it will be the two of us in this van.

I don't think I'll mind having time off so much anymore. I know we both need it.

Matt squeezes my hand, then lets go. He doesn't speak when he gets up, but I watch him move around our campsite, starting a fire and arranging ingredients for a meal. He banks fresh coals over the foil-wrapped potatoes. Next, he puts a cast iron pan on a grate over the flame. He unwraps the seasoned steak he's had in the cooler, then sets out onions and mushrooms he's going to cook afterwards.

"I want to do something nice for you after everything you've done for me."

He knows he doesn't have to do this, but don't try to stop him. I haven't had a home-cooked meal since the last time I visited Percilla.

The smell of the food cooking makes my mouth water and my stomach growl so loud, I think he can hear it because he looks at me with a big grin on his face.

"Come over here and let me make you a plate," he says.

I slide off the bed and put my sandals on, then take a seat at the picnic table.

"I've been thinking," he says, eyeing me warily.

"Yeah?"

"When are you planning to go back to work?"

I shrug, "I don't know yet."

I'm not sure how to tell him that Percilla and I haven't figured out what to do with him. We're not even sure how to give him a new life, and it feels strange to make that kind of choice for him without asking him first.

"When you do," he says, looking away, "can I go with you?"

I blink in surprise, because of all the things Percilla and I talked about, this wasn't one of them.

"I want to help," he says, filling the silence.

I open Tor on one of my black laptops and log in to SecureDrop. Percilla sent a new set of files. This case looks like a tough one. But as bad as it may be, I know we can handle it.

I copy the files to my flash drive and transfer them to the white laptop like I always do.

"On the plus side, this case doesn't have any children," I say, not bothering to look up as I do.

Matt sets a steaming cup of coffee down next to me, then sits on the edge of the bed.

"Is that for me?" I ask, hoping it is.

"Black with sugar."

"Thank you," I smile, blowing on the coffee before I take a sip. "It will be a good case for you to start with."

He smiles back, leaning in to watch what I'm doing.

"Are you nervous?"

"A little," he says, resting his elbows on his knees. "But I've got to rip the band-aid off sometime."

"The hardest part is always the first kill," I say, "but once you see what they're capable of, it becomes easier."

He nods, his brow furrowing.

"You don't have to do this if you don't want to. We could find somewhere to set you up. You can still have a normal life."

"No. I still want to know what happened to my family." He sounds sure of himself when he says it. "And if I took that deal, I might never find out."

Silence stretches between us, but I can tell there's something more he wants to say.

"I probably wouldn't get to see you anymore if I did that either."

I don't verbally agree with him even though I know it's true.

Even if I like having him around, I don't want to hold him back from the kind of life I'll never be able to have. I didn't have a choice, and he didn't before, but now he does.

"Hey," he says, interrupting my thoughts, "I want to do this… with you. You don't have to save everyone alone."

I blink hard, trying not to let my eyes fill with tears.

He touches my cheek, then pulls his hand away, looking embarrassed. We both try to look anywhere but at each other, and in such a small space, that's pretty challenging.

I clear my throat and put my hand on his knee, pushing past the awkwardness. "If you're sure this is what you really want, then we'll do it."

"Together."

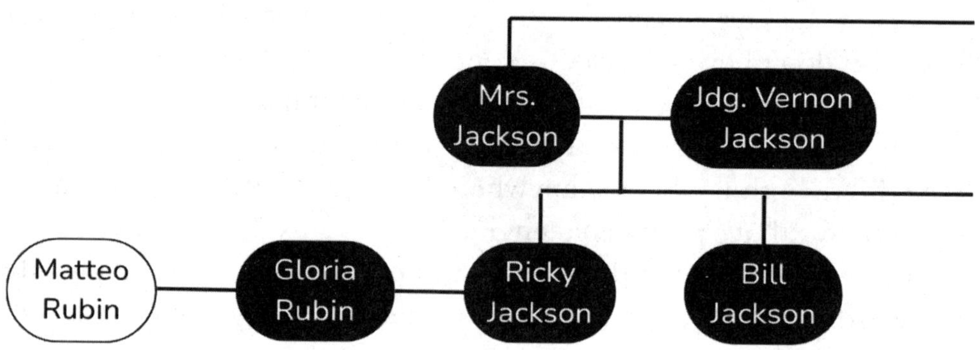
Mrs.
Jackson
Jdg. Vernon
Jackson
Matteo
Rubin
Gloria
Rubin
Ricky
Jackson
Bill
Jackson

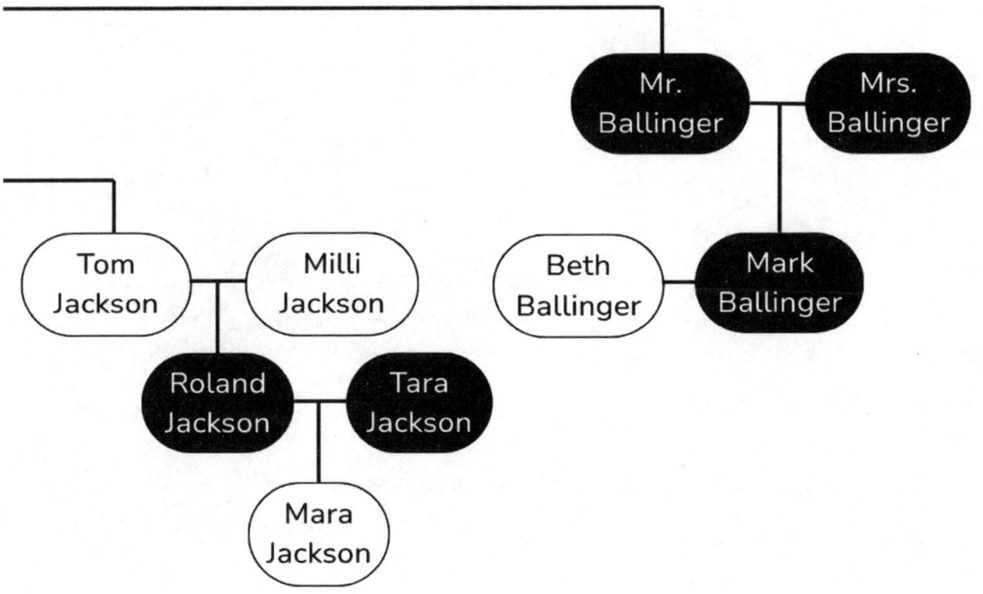
Mr. Ballinger
Mrs. Ballinger
Tom Jackson
Milli Jackson
Beth Ballinger
Mark Ballinger
Roland Jackson
Tara Jackson
Mara Jackson

BONUS CONTENT

TARA

I should have left when I had the chance. When Percilla told me it was too dangerous for her to help me. She recognized me from the start. Helped me get this place in Georgia, but said I shouldn't stay too long. A week was too long.

I wanted to take Mara to the beach. She loves it, and we've had a really good time, but today I swear I saw him when I was at the grocery store.

The lady at the daycare drop-off line looks at me funny when I pull back in with the parents who are running late.

"I'm sorry, Ms. Gates," I say, "I forgot Mara has a doctor's appointment. It's taken me forever to get her in."

She nods sympathetically, then turns to go get her.

I keep glancing in the rearview mirror for the dark vehicle I am sure is following me. I think I got away from them on the way here. I doubled back so many times I lost count.

Ms. Gates herds Mara back into the car, her pink backpack strap dragging on the ground behind her as she climbs into her booster seat.

"A doctor's appointment?" she asks as she buckles her seatbelt.

"But after, I promise we'll get ice cream," I say, forcing a smile.

She sighs the way only a five year old can to convey that she isn't happy about it, but my peace offering will do.

I pull out of line, but I haven't made it more than a block when I see the car again, three vehicles behind me. I loop around again, making several quick turns to get us closer to the house and further away from them. I should have kept the money on me, but as it is, we wouldn't make it a day with what I have left in my purse. And these groceries won't keep.

"Mommy, why are you driving like that?"

I glance in the mirror again, watching the car and catching a glimpse of my daughter's knit brow. "We're taking the fun way home."

"I don't like the fun way, and why are we going home? I thought you were taking me to the doctor. Am I sick?"

"You're not sick," I say, avoiding the rest of that minefield. "When we get to the house, Mara, I need you to be a good girl and listen to Mommy, okay?"

She nods.

When I haven't seen the car for five minutes, I pick back up my regular route for the last two blocks and pull up to the curb in front of the cottage.

There are no cars at the rest of the houses. I never noticed how lonely this street is during business hours. "Go inside and get your bag, okay? I'm right behind you."

I grab the groceries from the trunk and close the door behind me, then peek out the window. The car I spotted earlier is turning down my street.

I drop the grocery bags where I'm standing and lock the door, then turn the deadbolt.

"Mara," I say in a low tone. "Bring your bookbag and come here."

She rounds the corner from the kitchen, but doesn't ask any questions for maybe the first time in her life, and I can feel tears welling in my eyes because I'm sure she knows something is very wrong.

I open the coat closet door that is just behind the front door and dig into the pile of shoes, blankets, and coats that are stored there. Once I've cleared a spot, I pick up my daughter and hug her tight.

"Mommy, you're hurting me," she says.

I let her go and kiss her cheeks. "Be still and quiet for mamma, okay, baby? Promise me," I say, offering my pinky finger for her to twine her little one with, "no matter what you hear."

"I promise," she whispers.

Then I put her in the back corner of the closet, put her book bag on her lap and pile the things back in on top of her so all that's visible is a wall of blankets and coats. I close the closet door.

A car door slams outside in the driveway. I pick up the cordless phone in the kitchen and dial Percilla because I'm not sure if I can trust the police.

The phone rings three times before she answers. "He's here," I say.

Someone starts pounding on the door. I recognize his voice.

Roland.

"I have to go," I whisper. I don't hear what she says, just her voice in a haze of sound and the rain of blows against the front door.

"Tara," he shouts, "I know you're there! Open this fucking door!"

I leave the phone connected so no one can call in. I don't want him to find it, so I push it under the couch with my foot. And don't answer him shouting my name.

The front door shudders, and I can't tell if he's trying to kick it down or if he's driving into it with his shoulder. I back into the hallway.

The front door flies open.

Should I run? Try to draw him away from the house?

"Where is my daughter, Tara?" he asks.

"She's not here," I say, putting the couch between us.

He advances. "Tell me where she is!" He shoves past the couch, crowding me into the small living space with the glass coffee table and the cheap floral rug.

I'm already boxed in.

He reaches across the table, and I duck away from his grasp.

"What did you think was going to happen, Tara? Did you think I was going to let you take my daughter away from me? You were just going to get away without one word to me? I know you were snooping through that desk. I know you saw the papers. You're not stupid, but you stuck your nose where it didn't belong and then you ran."

"I know," I say, "I'm sorry. I should have said something." I climb over the back of the couch and run into the kitchen, tipping a dining chair over to block his path.

He chases after me, pushing it out of the way.

Something hits the back of my head with a crack. Glass shatters. I go down onto one knee. A burst of bright white pain shoots up my leg, and I gasp.

"Please don't hurt me," I say, knowing he has and he will again.

"Even if I wanted to let you go, do you think my family would let you be, knowing what you know? You're my responsibility, and I can't trust you."

I flip onto my back, curling my knees into my chest as he swings the dining chair down on me. I try not to scream. I don't want to frighten Mara anymore than I'm sure she already is. I'm so afraid she'll call out to me, come bursting out of the closet.

But she's quiet.

The chair crashes into me a second time, and the loose joint in the frame separates with a splintering crack as he hits me with it again. It ricochets off the edge of the couch and the bookcase that narrows the hall, softening the blow. He throws it away. It skitters down the hall and hits the wall.

I scoot backward on my elbows toward the open front door.

He kicks me hard once, twice, three times, and my lungs empty so completely I can't breathe in again. A shadow crosses over me. He slams the door. But the broken lock gives me a little hope that I might be able to make it outside to the yard. Maybe someone will be driving by and see me.

He kneels over me. "Tell me where my daughter is."

I shake my head as one of his hands closes around my throat.

My lungs burn.

The edges of my vision go fuzzy and gray.

His fist cracks into my face.

My lip splits, and I taste blood on my tongue.

He punches me again and again 'til I've lost count of the stinging blows and I feel a tooth crack, the inside of my lip slicing across its sharp edge.

My eyes start to swell shut.

He reaches into the back of his pants and takes out a gun. The cold steel striking my face is a new kind of pain.

"Look what you made me do, you fucking bitch." He lifts my head, smacking it into the floor.

I blink up at him, surprised at the air rushing back into my lungs. Blood pools at the back of my throat, and I gag.

"Where is my daughter?"

He shakes me, my head bouncing off the floor again.

"She's not here," I say, gasping for air. "she's at daycare."

He flips the gun around, pressing the barrel against my temple.

Tears burn my eyes, but I try to smile. "Please, Roland. I'm so sorry. I shouldn't have run away." My words are garbled through blood and swollen lips. I know it's too late, that my husband—the father of my child—is going to kill me.

The look in his eyes is a mix of rage and regret.

"Yeah, baby, you should have thought of that before you walked out on me."

He pulls the trigger.

The weight of him leaves my body. Hazy gray light flashes as he opens and closes the door, but he never looks in the closet. The adrenaline fades, and pain washes over me.

"Percilla, please protect my baby girl." My words sound garbled in my ears, more like incoherent moaning than anything else. I stop because I don't want to scare Mara.

I close my eyes.

"Mommy?" Mara's voice pulls me back.

I open my eyes, but I can't speak.
"Mommy, it's okay, I'm going to take care of you."

AUTHOR'S NOTE

I was younger than ten the first time one of my friends came to me and told me a little bit of what happened to them. It came out as a secret. I responded with a question. They told me they couldn't talk about it.

If I'd had a little more information, I would've known what to do. If I had known that talking to an adult would not have gotten us in trouble, I would've known how to help.

I was younger than fifteen when something happened to me. I was told that I should forgive that boy, because something happened to him, too. That was all there was to it.

So, this book is for you, and it's for me too. And for the rage you feel inside, you're not alone.

For those people who don't believe that children should be educated about their bodies, about details of things that can happen—let me tell you, the events in this book happen to the ones who don't know and are not protected. While the stories in these pages are not about one person and are fictitious, the facts are true.

These things happen to *real* people.

The scenarios, the injuries, the wounds, those are real and although they cannot be attributed to specific people in the real world, these characters hold the place of people who have lived through these kinds of trauma.

I tell this story for those who have not been able to speak because they were afraid, because there was no one safe to talk to, or because they didn't make it. I tell this story for myself and for the people around me, who did not have a voice.

ACKNOWLEDGMENTS

Thank you to my partner who has been so supportive. From making time for me to write on vacation, to coffee and snack runs. For building dedicated writing days into our schedules, and the tough love I need when I get distracted. You overlooked all the PC parts around the house and the printed drafts, pens, notebooks, and paper covering the dining table for weeks and never said a word about it. Thank you for all the times you bring me food and water and remind me that I need sleep.

Thank you to Troy, I could not have gone down this road without all the work we've done.

Natalie and Veronica, you are the very best writing partners a girl could ask for. You never fail to answer my random golfing questions and encourage me when I ask for the millionth time if I'm "doing too much." Thank you for holding me accountable to the promises I've made to myself and for being there with me every step of the way.

Mansion of Madness D&D group for gassing me up and getting me out of my own head.

To my Saturday walking buddy, April, thank you for getting me moving and letting me ramble about story ideas. You are the best.

To the bestest besties. Chuck, Hannah, and Nick, thank you for checking on me while I'm in my writing cave. Your love and support mean the world to me.

A big thank you to Dr. Susan Hoffman for being an early reader and providing all your valuable notes.

Thank you to Hal Meyer for helping me with a new PC build after my old one died, and I decided to fix it myself while on a writing deadline. What a time to do a complete teardown, deep clean, and rebuild. You saved me from myself.

Thank you to the online writing community. You have been so encouraging and supportive. Thanks for all the sprints.

Christian Storm, thank you for a beautiful cover, and going off finger-waving and vibes.

Thank you to Zara Hoffman and Inimitable Books for seeing the vision when *Mother Mercy* was little more than an idea and letting me tell the story in all its gory details. Thank you for letting me write about trauma my way.

ABOUT THE AUTHOR

Chandra Arthur is a Caribbean-American writer with her head in the clouds and her heart still on the beach in Barbados. An IT professional by day, she is the co-author of writing books in the *1,000 Words* series.

Mother Mercy is her solo fiction debut. She also writes science fiction, historical fiction, fantasy, and flash fiction stories.

She lives in Appalachia with her partner, their rescue dog Piper Prudence Maccon, their orange tabby cat Dobby Carlton III (there have been no others), and their three house plants.

When she isn't writing, you can find her pouring over a book, playing computer games, drinking coffee, and sometimes all three at once.

ALSO BY CHANDRA

1,000 Words **flash fiction writing prompt books**

1,000 Words to Get Started

1,000 Words to Ignite Romance

If you or a loved one are being abused, or feel like you might be in danger, please reach out to a trusted individual or a support network.

USA

National Domestic Violence Hotline
(all 50 states, Puerto Rico, Guam, US Virgin Islands)
1-800-799-SAFE (7233)
TTY: 1-800-787-3224
Video only (for deaf individuals): 1-206-518-9361

More information: *thehotline.org* (has a quick exit option)

Canada

Domestic Violence Resources
https://bit.ly/47XEnte